AR 5.1/5.0 pts.
Lexile: 810

D0232739

10-22R

SPY FORCE

mission:
In Search of the Time and Space Machine

Look for all of the

SPY FORCE
adventures

SPY FORCE

FORCE

mission:
In Search of the Time and Space Machine

BY DEBORAH ABELA · ILLUSTRATED BY GEORGE O'CONNOR
A Paula Wiseman Book · Simon & Schuster Books for Young Readers
New York   London   Toronto   Sydney

For Vera and Poz

SIMON & SCHUSTER BOOKS FOR YOUNG READERS
An imprint of Simon & Schuster Children's Publishing Division
1230 Avenue of the Americas, New York, New York 10020
Text copyright © 2002 by Deborah Abela
Illustrations copyright © 2005 by George O'Connor
Cover photograph copyright © Mike Brinson/Getty Images
First published in Australia in 2002 by Random House Australia Pty Ltd
Published by arrangement with Random House Australia Pty Ltd
First illustrated U.S. edition, 2005
All rights reserved, including the right of
reproduction in whole or in part in any form.
SIMON & SCHUSTER BOOKS FOR YOUNG READERS is a
trademark of Simon & Schuster, Inc.
Book design by Lucy Ruth Cummins
The text for this book is set in Goudy.
The illustrations for this book are rendered in ink.
Manufactured in the United States of America
10 9 8 7 6 5 4 3 2 1
CIP data for this book is available from the Library of Congress.
ISBN 978-1-4424-3085-3

Ah, there you are. Good. I was wondering when you were going to turn up. Where have you been? In fact, don't answer that. The life of a top spy is pretty busy and doesn't allow a lot of wriggle room when it comes to time. So let's get started.

My name is Max Remy. I live in New York with my mom, who is the head of publicity at a major television network, which means she spends most of her time running after the boring and famous. My mom is all style, stylists, and stars, and I can't stand any of it.

My dad lives with his new wife in California (which might as well be a million miles away) and is a filmmaker who would spend heaps more time with me if he could. He's busy too.

The only other family we have is my mom's sister, Aunt Eleanor, and her husband, Ben, who live on a chicken farm. We never see them, which is probably good. I don't think I'd be any good with chickens. And I <u>know</u> I'm no good with dogs. All that fur. Urghh. As for friends, every time I made a new friend, we'd have to move because Mom or Dad would get a new job, so I figured it was better not to make any in the first place. Saves on all those messy good-byes.

Anyway, time's run out. I have to get back to Alex. She has a mission to complete and a world to save. See ya!

<u>Max Remy</u>

CHAPTER 1

Dr. Evilbrain
Strikes Again

Chronicles of Spy Force:

Time: 2:45 P.M.

Date: Friday afternoon, somewhere in the future

Place: Spy Force Headquarters

Dr. Evilbrain was in the middle of another evil plan to destroy the world and the Chief of Spy Force had his top spy, Alex Crane, on the case as the only one who could stop him.

Dr. Evilbrain was the world's greatest mastermind of evil. He was responsible for feats of evil that other evildoers only dreamed of. He was Spy Force's most wanted archenemy, and Spy Force would not rest until the world was free of him.

Not only that, he was just about the ugliest person who was ever popped out into the world.

He had one thick eyebrow that dripped down his brow and into the edges of his eyes, which were small and beady like two rats sniffing for food from inside a dark hole. His nose was a mess of acne scars that looked like someone had taken a piece of the moon and stuck it right in the middle of his face. The ugly stick had been waved so high and long above his head, that on the day he was born, his own mother ran from the hospital and never wanted to see him again. He was so repulsive, mosquitoes wouldn't bite him and mirrors didn't crack when they saw him—they cried out in fear of their lives.

1

There was only one way to say it.

Dr. Evilbrain wasn't pretty.

And he wasn't stupid, either. At least he wasn't stupid after he'd had the operation. He had the most villainous brain that ever slimed its way into a human head.

Literally.

Dr. Evilbrain had created the world's first synthetic brain, equipped with hypersmart intelligence and precision evil, and he knew that with this brain, he'd be smart enough to take over the world. In a complex and very sloppy operation, his assistant, the sinister Count Igor, cut open Dr. Evilbrain's head, scooped out his squelchy old brain, and replaced it with his new and slimy smart one.

That's when Dr. Evilbrain hatched his latest plan.

With his new brain squishing around in his head, Dr. Evilbrain developed algae that would, in just twenty-four hours, multiply and choke the world's water supply of its oxygen, killing all living things and making water supplies everywhere poisonous for people to drink.

Human life would have only weeks to live.

For most people, it wouldn't even be that long.

It was up to Alex Crane, the world's greatest mastermind against evildoers, to create an antidote that would kill the algae and stop the deadly countdown to the end of the world.

She'd been working for twenty-two hours straight. There were only two hours left. All she needed was to add

2

one drop of her secret ingredient and get down to the shores of the ocean before the deadline was up.

But only a drop.

Just one more . . .

Kaboom!!

⊕

Great sticky clumps of green slime went everywhere. Oozing down walls, across desks, soaking through books, and, worst of all, covering Max from the top of her head down to her brand new shoes.

She wiped the slime from her eyes and realized she wasn't Alex Crane, Superspy, but Max Remy of Class 6B, and her mom was really going to give it to her this time.

A sea of kids' faces traffic-jammed around her, laughing at her new look. Members of Class 6B were not known for their subtlety, and they weren't about to change now.

"Hey brainiac, can't you use a tissue like everyone else?"

"What's the matter, feeling a little green?"

"Guess who forgot to have a bath today?"

The room exploded in a deafening roar of laughter. Suddenly everyone was a comedian. Even Ms. Ellen got in on the act.

"Okay, class, that's enough. Max has just had a little accident," she said. But Max could see that Ms. Ellen was only just managing to hold back her own laugh.

"Even though green really is your color, Max."

That was it.

You'd think that it was the funniest joke anyone had ever made in the history of the entire world. Max wanted every bird there was to fly over Ms. Ellen's head and slime her with their smelly poo. She imagined her teacher running around with her new poo-dropping hairdo, screaming and trying to get it off.

It was as if Ms. Ellen could read Max's thoughts because her face turned serious and she lowered her voice.

"Max, one of the most important lessons we can learn is not to take ourselves too seriously. Otherwise, you'll be sixty-five before you realize you've never had a really good laugh."

Just then the bell rang.

Phew! Saved from any more of Ms. Ellen's women's magazine philosophies.

The class let out a big cheer and Ms. Ellen could only just be heard.

"Have a good, safe summer vacation everyone and I'll see you next year," she called out.

Kids swarmed everywhere, trying to grab their bags and get out the door—freedom at last.

For Max, this meant relief from the halfwits she had to sit next to.

Adios and see you later. She was out of there, and as far as she was concerned, nothing beat the fact that she wouldn't have to see any of the other kids' lame, laughing faces for the entire summer.

"Ah, Max?"

It was Ms. Ellen.

Max's foot was almost out the door.

"Yes?" she replied.

"You're not going to leave without cleaning up this mess, are you?" asked Ms. Ellen with her eyebrows raised so high that Max thought they'd fly off her forehead.

Max looked at the green slime–covered desk, floor, and walls. Cleaning it up would take practically all summer.

"I didn't think so," said Ms. Ellen, collecting her books and papers. "Now, don't forget to have some fun on vacation, and I'll see you much more relaxed and happy next year."

It took every ounce of Max's self-control not to pick up some slime and put it through her teacher's roller-curled hair. Instead, she imagined Ms. Ellen as a giant bug-eyed monster with horrible breath and cockroaches crawling out of her nose.

"Yes, Ms. Ellen," she said, smiling.

After she'd finished cleaning up, Max got her bag and went into the corridor where the other kids were waiting for her.

Especially Toby Jennings and his little fan club.

"So Max, having a little trouble with your funny bone?" said Toby.

"Maybe you should have it looked into?" droned one of his followers.

"Maybe when you were born, they forgot to give you one," said another.

Max ignored them, trying to get to the main door and out of the building as soon as possible.

They wouldn't let it rest. But it was Toby who really knew how to get at her.

"So Miss Enormous Brain, had a little slime trouble today?"

Max was good at science, but Toby was better at exams and always just beat her. And he let her know it.

"Looks like your second place behind me wasn't a terrible mistake after all, Ms. Einstein."

Max's head was alive with what felt like a hundred snakes wanting to jump out and slither all over Toby, squeezing him to silence.

The snakes never appeared, so Toby kept on mouthing off.

"I knew you were the queen of slime, but I didn't think you were into making it," he sneered.

Now the other kids really let loose.

Max tried to walk past them.

"What's the matter, slime got your tongue?"

Max never understood why Toby Jennings didn't just

6

turn into a toad and fall into the nearest swamp with all the other crawling creatures.

She had had enough. She didn't have to take this anymore. But just as she was about to let him have it, a piece of slime wormed its way out of her hair, down her forehead, and onto her nose.

This was just what Toby needed for his final blow.

"Ah! It's alive," he screamed. "The slime's coming out of her brain. It's coming to get us all. Run for your lives! Aaaahhhhhh!"

The corridor burst into a riot of screaming kids falling and laughing and running as fast as they could to get away from Max and her slime brain, as if they had just been told that the world were going to self-destruct in five seconds.

Which wouldn't be such a bad idea. At least then Max would never have to come back to this school and all the lame-brained students who went there.

The corridor was clear in ten seconds flat. Good riddance. All Max had to do was get her bag, walk out those doors, and she wouldn't have to step back in this place for a whole summer.

But there was one thing she'd forgotten.

Her mom.

Max met her on the steps.

"What happened to you?" she gasped. "What's that in your hair? And what have you done to your new shoes?"

Of course, the shoes. It felt like things always seemed

much more important to her mom than Max was.

"What will it take to teach you a little respect for your things, young lady?"

Normally Max would have had a great comeback. Something funny and sharp. She was pretty good at those. But she was feeling sticky from the slime that was starting to harden and smell like she'd just fallen down the ickiest toilet in the world.

Max had to get away from the sniggering she could still hear behind her.

"I don't know, Mom. Let's just get out of here."

CHAPTER 2

A Million Miles from Hollywood...

Max climbed in the car with her mom and said nothing. As they drove away, she could hear the chanting of "slime lady" slowly recede behind them as they moved farther away from the school.

Her mother sat staring ahead, gripping the steering wheel like she was trying to squeeze it into another shape. But Max knew that the silence wasn't going to last long.

"What's gotten into you lately?" said Max's mom in her at-her-wits'-end voice.

Max also knew that when a conversation started this way it never got any better.

"Nothing," said Max.

"Don't tell me 'nothing.' The last few weeks you've been moody, you've barely said a word, and I can't remember the last time I saw you really smile."

"Why is everyone so concerned about me being Ms. Smiley?" Max exploded.

"Everyone who?" asked her mom.

"Doesn't matter," Max said, and sank down lower into her seat to the crunch of plastic bags her mom had laid out so Max's slimed clothes wouldn't wreck the upholstery.

"Yes, it matters. It's like you don't care for anything anymore. You used to be such a happy girl, always off playing with other kids, but now it's like you don't want to have anything to do with anyone," and here there was a well-timed pause before her mother added, "including me."

"Well, you don't have to worry about that much

longer," said Max, perking up. "As soon as Dad picks me up tomorrow, I'll be out of your hair for the summer."

Max's mother faced the road and, although it seemed impossible, gripped the wheel even harder. Her voice softened.

"Actually, there's been a change of plans."

The way her mother said it, Max knew these new plans weren't a good thing.

"What change of plans?" she asked suspiciously.

"Your father has been offered a very important film to direct and won't be able to come back to New York this year."

Max's dad lived in Los Angeles, and her mother wanted nothing to do with him after he fell in love with a famous actress and moved to California, where the weather is always sunny and people are tanned and sit around in cafes all day. Even though it sounded like a really boring way to live, compared to spending the summer in her mother's company, it would be heaven.

"But we all agreed that Dad was going to come here for his vacation!" Max cried.

"Sweetie, this is a big opportunity for your father and it was a really hard decision for him. I know it doesn't seem fair . . ."

"Well, if he can't come here, I'll go to California and be with him," Max said, trying not to cry. "I'm old enough to fly by myself, and I'd have much more fun staying with

Dad and his new wife than I will staying here."

Max knew this would hurt her mother, but she said it anyway.

"Now, Max, your father's going to be too busy to look after you. You know that when he directs he has no time for anybody. . . ."

Max looked away and mumbled into the window.

"If you'd made more time to be with us instead of your dumb job, maybe Dad wouldn't have left us in the first place."

Max jerked forward as her mother pulled over to the side of the road and stopped the car.

Her eyes shifted toward her mother's beet-red face, which always meant one thing. She was really going to get it now.

"Look, Max, I know it's hard for you to understand, but what happened between your father and me was very complicated. I know you think it's my fault that we got divorced, but there was a lot more involved than you know about."

"Like what?" asked Max.

"When you're older, you and I will sit down and have a long talk about it, but for now you're too young and you just wouldn't understand," said Max's mom, softening her voice.

Max looked away. She hated it when her mother treated her like a kid.

"Please, Max, we don't have time to talk now. We have to get you home so you can pack."

Max turned sharply.

"Pack for where?" she asked.

Her mom took a deep breath.

"For the farm. It's been arranged that you'll spend summer vacation with Uncle Ben and Aunt Eleanor. They're expecting us tonight."

Uncle Ben and Aunt Eleanor! The same Uncle Ben and Aunt Eleanor who lived in the country, a million miles from anywhere? Who spent their days raising sheep and stomping through cow manure? The thought of spending her vacation with this pair of country bumpkins was as horrifying as being locked in a cage with giant, human-eating spiders! And as exciting as being strapped to a chair and watching mud dry on their worn-out cowhide boots.

Really, really boring!

Suddenly, being with her mother didn't seem so bad after all.

"Why can't I stay with you?" Max pleaded.

"Because things are really busy for me now, and I think it would be better if you got out of the city for a while and breathed some fresh country air. The city is no place for a twelve-year-old to spend a summer."

Max sat staring out the windshield at the city. She felt like she was seeing it for the last time, convinced that if she was made to go to the farm, boredom would take hold of her within days and leave her a shivering, zombied mess.

She hated the country, and she hated even more the idea

of spending it with two chicken farmers she barely knew.

Her mother leaned over and stroked her cheek.

"I realize this is hard for you Max, but you know I love you. I've certainly been busy lately, and these last few years without Dad have been hard on the both of us, but it will get better. I promise."

Max's mother gave her a quick kiss and started the car.

"We'd better get going," she said, looking at her watch.

Max wiped the kiss away and crossed her arms against her chest.

Her mom worked in the publicity department of a major TV station and her life was full of dinners, openings, famous people, and parties. It seemed pretty cushy to Max, and as they drove on in silence, she knew she was the one with the hard life.

CHAPTER 3

The End of the World

Chronicles of Spy Force:

This was one of the hardest assignments yet for Alex Crane.

She'd been captured and was being driven to the secret hideout of the infamous Camilla La Koole, the most notorious mastermind of poisons the world had ever seen. Camilla's cunning plans saw her befriend the rich and famous and, when they least expected it, spray them with her poisons. Each poison was enough to keep the person immobile until she could steal their riches and escape.

And when her victims awoke, they remembered nothing.

Camilla was the richest and cleverest woman the underworld had ever known, and Spy Force had Alex Crane on the case to bring her evil ways to an end.

Of course, Alex wasn't really captured. She'd let Camilla trap her and, armed with a Spy Force microrecorder in her watch and a piece of Truth Gum, which, when chewed, forced the chewer to tell the truth, she'd trick Camilla into confessing all.

Just one piece of gum.

⊕

Max's head was thrown forward and her pen skidded across the page as the car came to an abrupt stop. A cattle dog had run onto the road and her mother had seen it just in time to stop.

Max wasn't superspy Alex Crane in some exotic spy

19

location anymore. She was Max Remy and she was in Mindawarra, Pennsylvania. A town that had one diner, a Chinese restaurant, a police station, and a general store with a couple of gas pumps out front. The only person in sight was an old man asleep on the bench at a bus stop that looked like there hadn't been a bus through for about a hundred years.

This was Mindawarra. Max's home for the entire summer vacation.

"According to this, Ben and Eleanor's farm is about two miles east of here," said her mom, poring over a map. "So it won't be long now."

Long until what? Max thought. Until she became comatose with boredom as she spent the summer watching cows graze? *Great.*

The sun was just starting to set when they pulled onto a dirt road and, after two dusty, potholed miles, came upon a house that looked like something out of a horror film: broken down, creaky, and smothered by evil-looking trees. The only person who could possibly feel at home here was some half-crazed lunatic who'd had his brain removed at birth.

Ben and Eleanor came rushing out to meet them. Max almost got smothered in the folds of clothes as Eleanor swooped down on her and gave her a hug. She untangled herself, lucky to escape alive.

Ben stepped toward Max's mother and the two exchanged a brief handshake.

20

"Hello," they both said coolly.

Max's mother wiped her hand with a hanky as if to wipe the handshake away. She then mumbled a quick hello to her sister and what sounded like a quiet "Thank you."

"Would you like to stay for dinner?" asked Eleanor.

"No, thanks. I really should be going. I'm late already." Then she turned to Max. "Bye, sweetie. Anything you need, just call me. Okay? I'll see you in August. I love you."

And with that she was gone. A small cloud of dust followed her car out the front gate and back to the city.

Back to the real world.

Eleanor picked up Max's bags.

"Come on, Max. I'll show you to your room," she said cheerily.

Max followed Eleanor and only just missed stepping on dog doo before walking up the creaky, dusty front steps.

At the top she turned and looked around her. There wasn't another house in sight. This really was the end of the world, and she'd been farmed out like some dumb animal to graze with a couple of hillbillies. Max pictured herself as an old woman walking off the farm, fat from years of eating steak and potatoes every night and watching cows wander around dusty paddocks.

She jumped back as a chicken flapped past her as if from nowhere. She covered her face with her arms as it landed and then cackled like it was having a good laugh at her.

"You won't think it's so funny when you're next Sunday's lunch," she snapped.

Max stepped onto the verandah that circled the house and then through the screen door that slammed closed behind her. Inside, she couldn't believe what she saw. She was standing in a long, dark corridor that led all the way through the house to the kitchen at the end. Cobwebs dangled from lights that looked like they were from the last century. As she stepped foreward carefully, she looked into the living room to her left and stared open-mouthed at its giant sofas, bare wooden floor, and creepy pictures of really old people propped up on a mantelpiece that looked like it took all its strength just to stay up. Through frayed curtains, a large window let in streaks of grayish light like frozen lightning bolts. There were bookshelves lining almost every wall and a large glass cabinet that contained some old ornaments, yellowing papers, and books left over from the Dark Ages. A tall lamp stood in the corner like a skinny man with a large hat and nowhere to go, while a squat table nestled underneath it.

But that wasn't the worst of it.

There was no TV. What kind of a house had no TV?

"Max, I'm in here."

Max followed Eleanor's voice out of the TV-less living room.

Then she saw something she really couldn't believe. Her room. That's what Eleanor called it anyway. It wasn't a proper room but a bed on the back verandah. The "sleep-out" they called it, and Eleanor showed it to Max like it was the most special room in the whole place. At least here she'd be able to make a quick getaway in the middle of the night if the whole relic of a house fell down around them.

"I'll leave you here to get settled in. Dinner will be ready in about twenty minutes," said Eleanor.

Max looked around the sleep-out.

"Thanks, but I'm not hungry. I think I'll just go to bed early."

Eleanor smiled, but Max could tell she was disappointed.

"Good night, then. We'll see you in the morning," she said, and closed the door behind her.

Max wondered what a great spy would do to get out of this situation. How would she plan her escape? In the middle of nowhere and trapped in a house with no TV.

Max changed into her pajamas and slid into bed. She could hear Eleanor and Ben laughing in the kitchen, that is when they weren't singing off-key and talking at the top of their voices.

She pulled the blankets over her head and thought about her dad in Los Angeles. She missed him and wondered why he was always too busy to spend time with her. She turned over in her squeaky bed and wished she were at home, with its flat screen TV, cozy living room, and bed with soft, comfortable pillows.

Eventually Ben and Eleanor quieted down, and the lights in the house were turned off.

Just as Max was about to fall asleep, she heard a noise. It was like an animal sniffing at the door of the verandah, only inches from where she was asleep. The hinges creaked as the door opened slowly. Max held her breath as she thought of who it might be. Maybe it was some terrible monster or a raving lunatic who lived deep in the country and only came out at night.

In the moonlight Max saw an old baseball bat on the floorboards near her bed. She moved slowly, trying not to be heard but the squeaking springs of the bed were like a hungry cat that wouldn't be quiet. She reached out and picked up the bat, sitting bolt upright in bed, ready to strike.

Then she heard footsteps. She had to tell herself to take another breath; she was so scared she'd stopped breathing.

Then she saw the silhouette of a large figure and heard the sound of heavy boots trying to be quiet as they stepped toward her.

Closer and closer.

This was it, thought Max. *I'm going to die!*

A madman had broken into the house and was coming to get her. Max could hardly hear her own thoughts, her heart was beating so loudly in her chest.

She was done for. She could see the headlines now: "Girl disappears from farm without a trace." For years police would try and solve the mystery of her disappearance. Her mother would sob and sob and make sure her makeup was on properly before the TV news team interviewed her about her lost child. But what she'd forget to say is that it was her idea to send Max away in the first place, even though Max had begged to stay with her. If she did disappear, her mom wouldn't have to worry about cooking her dinner, or coming home early, or Max's new shoes that she'd wrecked. Life would be great for her mom. No more Max to worry about, just all those famous people and a life full of parties.

Then the screen door opened and the footsteps receded into the night.

Phew! She was safe. For now. But who knew when the lunatic would be back or if there were more of them hiding in the bushes, ready to steal into the night and scare innocent children.

Max got out of bed and snuck to the window. She watched the beam of a flashlight as it made its way to a small shed. A light was turned on inside the shed, and she could see the black silhouette of a man. Who was he and what was he doing? Maybe he was a crazed psychopath creating a devastating device of evil. Maybe he was no better than Dr. Evilbrain and it was up to Max to stop him before he destroyed the world.

Max climbed into bed and gripped the bat firmly, just in case she needed it. She lay there staring at the door and listening to every rustle, hoot, and buzzing sound that filled the night air. The end of summer vacation seemed a very long way away. Finally she fell asleep.

CHAPTER 4

Mud Monsters and
Savage Wolves

Chronicles of Spy Force:

Superspy Alex Crane was being pursued by the treacherous Baron Lichtenstein and his hungry pack of wolves. Alex had uncovered the Baron's scheme of smuggling top-secret Government plans out of the country in a collection of talking dolls, and was now running for her life with the Baron and his wolves in hot pursuit. Just as Alex was about to pass through the gates of the Baron's estate to safety, she tripped and sprained her ankle. She tried to stand up but the pain was too great. The wolves were gaining on her fast. She could hear the Baron's laugh of victory as they were about to pounce.

Was this the end of Alex Crane? Would the wolves eat her alive? Would Spy Force lose its greatest spy ever?

⊕

Max woke up in terror. Someone had thrown something large and woolly over her and was trying to smother her. She struggled beneath the furry weight, trying to breathe, trying to scream, fighting for her life. Maybe it was the heavy-footed man who had terrorized her last night and had come back to kill her. Or maybe it was her weird uncle and aunt who wanted to chop her up and feed her to the chickens. She knew they were crazy. Probably crazy enough to kill.

They weren't going to do me with her that easily, thought

Max. She struggled, using all her strength against the smothering weight. Then she felt a long wet slap across her face. What was that? Then she heard a bark.

A dog! It was a dog!

"Get off me!" she screamed. "I said, get off me!"

Max gave the dog one big shove and it landed on the floor next to her bed. But it thought she was playing and jumped back up on her again.

"Will somebody get rid of this maniac dog before he kills me!" she yelled.

Eleanor came into the room and laughed as she pulled the dog off Max.

"Ralph, I know you're excited to have a new guest in the house, but at least let her wake up before you say good morning," said Eleanor.

Max was furious that Eleanor thought it was so funny. She'd almost been killed! Eleanor wouldn't be laughing if she'd found her lying blue in the face with her eyes wide open, having taken her last dog-smelling breath.

"Sorry about that. Ralph was only trying to be friendly," said Eleanor apologetically.

"Well, I'd appreciate it if you controlled your dog so I'm not attacked every morning when I wake up," Max said sharply.

Eleanor looked hurt.

Max wiped the dog spit from her face and brushed dog hairs off her pajamas.

"He didn't mean any harm, but I'll make sure he sleeps outside from now on."

Ralph gave a yelp. Eleanor wouldn't really leave him outside all night, would she? Not after all these years. Besides, he hated being alone in the dark.

"Come on, Ralph. Let's leave Max to get dressed in peace," said Eleanor. Ralph looked away from Max, let out a small whimper, and, with his tail sagging to the floor, he quietly left the room after his mistress.

Max threw off the blankets in one angry sweep. Finding her slippers under the bed, she took her toothbrush and dog-smelling self to the bathroom. When she got there, she stood in the doorway with her mouth open as she looked at what was to pass for a bathroom for the next months. It was a small room with one window up high and a small cracked mirror that hung even higher from a crooked nail. Even hardened criminals had it better than this, she thought.

The walls were a floral mess of pale pink and green tiles that looked like they had come straight out of a magazine from the 1950s. Tiles had fallen off the walls and were piled on a shelf, waiting to be fixed. The bathroom cabinet was so small Max wondered that anything could fit in it, and the toilet lid looked heavy enough to break her arm just trying to lift it up. The bath was so deep she thought she was going to need a ladder just to get in, and above it the shower nozzle poked out from the wall like a miniature

31

metal weapon left over from the war. Around the bath hung a bright yellow curtain splattered with ducks and rainbows.

Nothing matched, nothing was her height, everything was a nightmare.

As Max tried to get up the courage to enter the room, she thought of her mother. There was a lot about her Max didn't like, but one thing she did have was a sense of style, which Eleanor must have missed when they were handing it out.

"Why me?" muttered Max. She took a deep breath and stepped through the doorway, wanting to wash away every trace of the smelly dog as quickly as possible.

After cleaning up, Max felt better, but when she got to the kitchen she met her next horror.

Breakfast!

Eleanor smiled as she saw Max enter the room.

"Just in time," she said, as she placed before Max a plate of fried eggs, bacon, toasted white bread, and a large mug of tea.

Max gulped hard trying to imagine eating it all.

Unlike the bathroom, the kitchen was a big room with light pouring in from the yard. There were cupboards everywhere. The benches and shelves were cluttered with jam jars, sauce bottles, biscuit tins, recipe books, and canisters with tea, flour, and sugar written on them. There was a spice rack with what looked like every spice in the world and a walk-in pantry that was filled from the floor to the ceiling with boxes, tins, packets, and containers. The floor was like a giant checkerboard of linoleum, and right in the middle was a high wooden table covered with jars of spreads, a jug of milk, cups, a pot of tea, a large loaf of bread, a sugar pot, some cereal boxes, a toaster, knives, forks, and spoons, egg cups shaped like miniature Humpty Dumpty characters, and, nestled right in the middle of it all, a small vase of flowers. Max's eyes fell on the plate in front of her.

"Thanks, but I'm not hungry," she said.

"Not hungry? Rubbish," said Ben, sliding his toast through the yellow egg goo on his plate. "You didn't have dinner last night. You must be hungry."

"It's just that I usually have freshly squeezed juice and fruit salad for breakfast," explained Max.

"That's not enough to keep a young girl growing big and strong," her uncle scoffed as he kept eating and Max noticed him give Eleanor a quick wink. "Besides, you'll need extra energy to work around the farm."

Work around the farm? Big and strong? Not only was she sentenced to spending her holidays miles from any kind of civilization, but she was also going to be used in child labor. Knowing she had no choice, Max sat at the table, scraped the butter off her toast, and made a mental note to call the child welfare authorities as soon as she could.

Just then the screen door slammed and there stood the gangliest boy with the wildest hair she'd ever seen.

"I've given Ralph a talking to and left him outside," he said.

Her uncle swallowed the final piece of his egg goo combo.

"Linden, this is Max. She's staying for the summer and needs to be shown around the place. Think you can do it?" said Ben.

"No problem. What's the weather going to be?" asked Linden.

"Larry's been digging holes like there's no tomorrow, so I'd say we are in for a good drenching tonight," Ben forecast.

This was too much for Max. Who was Larry and what did digging holes have to do with rain?

Eleanor noticed Max's confusion.

"Larry's our pig. We can tell the weather by how he behaves."

Linden saw Max needed more convincing.

"He's only been wrong two times before and that was because he had a cold."

Now Max knew she was living in the Land of the Loonies.

"Right. I'm off," said Ben, wiping his mouth. He walked over to Eleanor, picked her up under the arms and gave her the sloppiest kiss Max had ever seen two married people give each other. Yuck! She looked away and waited for them to stop.

Eleanor straightened herself out.

"I'll see you all about lunchtime and not before. I've got lots to do and could do with some peace around the house."

Max was skeptical. Lots of work? How hard could it be to scrub floors and feed chickens? At least being with Wildboy would be more interesting than being indoors cleaning out cupboards.

Outside, Linden called Ralph who ran quickly toward him.

"Oh, so the horse is yours?" asked Max.

"No, he belongs to Eleanor and Ben," Linden explained. "But he stays at my place two nights a week. He won't be any problem. You won't even know he's around."

"You bet I won't because I'm going my own way," said Max, turning on her heels.

"But Ben asked me to show you around," said Linden.

"I think I can show myself around." And with that, Max was off. She wasn't going to spend any more time than she had to with Farmer Brown Jr. She'd make her own fun.

But it was later, while Max was in the back paddock, that she found herself in trouble.

She'd been walking through the tall grass cursing the day she was driven to this wasteland. Flies buzzed around her face and up her nose. No matter how many times she swished them away, her favorite T-shirt was being snagged by scrubby bushes, and burrs stuck their gnarly prickles into her new baggy pants. When she stopped to try and get them out, she found herself ankle-deep in mud.

"Yuck! Swampland. Just what I should have expected," she said out loud.

When she tried to lift one foot, she sank a little deeper. And when she tried lifting the other, that got her even further into trouble.

Now Max really started to worry. Every time she moved, she sank deeper into the brown smelly slime. She tried again to lift one foot out, but this time she became unbalanced and fell forward into the mud. She put out her hands to break her fall, but all she felt were a few sticks and rocks floating in the stinky mess and no solid ground. She was really done for now. What would Alex Crane do in this situation?

"You need a hand?" said a voice behind her.

Max twisted around. Great! Just my luck. I get stuck in some mud and Country Boy and his hound turn up out of nowhere. She could hear him now, laughing at her and calling her the mud queen, just like all the kids at school would have done, making sure everyone within a two-hundred-mile radius knew about it. And making jokes like, "How does someone get a pat on the head? Sit under a cow." All the corny ones Toby Jennings would have let fly by now.

"No. I'm fine, thanks," she said stubbornly.

Linden offered his hand.

"Come on. You'll never get out of there without help."

"I can do it by myself," Max insisted.

"Okay. Whatever you say. I'll be here if you need me," said Linden.

He pushed his hair out of his eyes and watched as Max struggled with the mud and cowpats and bits of tree and other things that squelched around her. She tried to find solid ground, but only managed to sink deeper into the filth.

The stuff was up to her waist when she really started to panic.

"Well, don't just stand there," she yelled. "Help me!"

Linden picked up a long, sturdy stick and held it out to her over the oozing mess. Ralph stood on the edge of the mud and supervised the whole operation.

"Wow! You're heavier than I thought," gasped Linden.

"Just get me out of here," said Max, losing her temper.

When she was freed from the mud pool, she looked like a giant chocolate stick.

Linden couldn't help but smile. Max did look pretty funny.

"I'll walk you back to the farm," he said, trying to keep himself from laughing.

"I can go by myself," said Max, scraping great clumps of mud from her clothes.

"I was going there anyway. It's almost lunchtime," offered Linden.

Great! Now she had to walk with him all the way to the farm, where he'd laugh as he told her uncle and aunt how stupid she was, getting stuck in the mud. Max folded her muddied arms across her even muddier chest, and walked a few paces ahead of him.

Some vacation this is going to be, she thought.

"So where are you from?" asked Linden.

What was it going to take for Country Bumpkin to realize that Max wasn't interested in any of his chatter? She walked on in silence, hoping he'd get the message.

He tried again. "How come you're spending your vacation here?"

This kid just wasn't getting it.

"Let's just get to the house," said Max dismissively.

"I was just asking . . ."

Max swung around, put her muddy hands on her muddy hips and really gave it to him.

"Listen, Farmboy, I'm here because I have to be, not because I want to be, and just because you got me out of that mud hole doesn't mean I have to talk to you or anyone else if I don't want to. And guess what? I don't want to! In fact, the only thing I really want is the quickest way off this farm. So let's just get back to the house as soon as we can, so I can wash this mud from my skin before it soaks into my head and starts eating my brain."

38

Linden sighed as he watched Max walk away.

Sometimes girls were hard to understand.

Ralph barked as if he were thinking the same thing.

As Max squelched through the grass, she thought about inventing today's new spy adventure. And here she was covered in mud in someplace that probably wasn't even on the map.

Suddenly Linden and Max heard an enormous explosion. Max flung herself on the ground and covered her head.

"What was that?" she mumbled into the dirt.

Linden stared down at Max as she lay at his feet.

"That's Ben. Working," he explained.

"Working? What's he doing, blowing up cows?" Max asked.

"Cows?" Linden looked confused.

"Yeah. That's what farmers do, don't they? Work with cows?" Max asked.

This time Linden couldn't hold back and let out a really good laugh.

"A farmer? Ben? He wouldn't know the front of a cow from the back unless I pointed it out to him."

Max clenched her teeth. She hated being laughed at, and she thought she might look a little ridiculous lying in the dirt so she stood up.

"If he's not a farmer, what does he do?" she demanded.

"He's a scientist, of course. So is Eleanor. They *are* your aunt and uncle, aren't they?" asked Linden.

Max was a bit embarrassed.

"Our families aren't really close," she explained. "And if they are scientists, why aren't they working in some laboratory somewhere?"

Linden looked around him.

"We're in the middle of nowhere," Max said bitingly. "I'm pretty sure no one's going to hear us."

"Okay, but what I'm about to tell you is top secret."

The way Linden said it made Max even more curious. "Sure." She swished away a very stubborn blowfly. "Now tell me before I get eaten alive."

Linden lowered his voice. "They used to, in England. They were part of a team of top scientists working for the British government, but they left it all behind and came to America. They owned expensive cars, were earning loads of money and winning awards with everything they did, but now Ben works in his shed all times of the day and night. I guess working for the government wasn't all it was cracked up to be."

So that could explain the footsteps on the verandah last night, Max thought.

"What are they working on now?" she asked.

"Eleanor sends articles to scientific journals and has written heaps of books, and Ben is working on a secret project that could change the face of the world as we know it," said Linden proudly.

Max had to get this straight. The same Ben who wiped

toast through egg goo and the same Eleanor who thought you could tell the weather by the behavior of a pig were brilliant scientists from England? Things were really turning out to be stranger than she thought they ever could be.

"What's the secret project?" she asked.

"He said he couldn't tell us until he was finished, but he reckons that could be any day now."

"Can we have a look?" asked Max, still skeptical about what Linden was saying.

"He doesn't like to be interrupted," explained Linden.

Max wanted to check out what this top secret project was, so she pushed a little further.

"Shouldn't we make sure he's okay?" she asked.

"He'll be fine. Happens all the time," said Linden.

If Ben really was working on a project that would change the world, Max wasn't going to waste her time falling into swamps. She was going to find out all about it. But first she needed a shower. The flies were beginning to buzz around her in swarms, and the drying mud was really starting to stink.

CHAPTER 5

What You See Is Not Always What You Get

When Max and Linden arrived at the farm, there was no one in the kitchen making lunch.

"Eleanor's probably gone to get Ben," said Linden. "Once he starts working he can forget that the world's still turning."

Linden paused, staring toward the shed as if he were gazing at some ancient wonder. Max rolled her eyes. After a few seconds, Linden turned to her and realized he must have looked a little odd.

"That's what Eleanor says, anyway."

"Right," said Max, and walked away. She wasn't interested in anything Farmboy had to say. All she needed now was a hot shower. By now the mud had dried, making it hard for Max to move. She walked down the hall with her legs bowed, like she'd just got off a horse. She stopped in front of Ben and Eleanor's prehistoric bathroom.

"I bet cavemen had better bathrooms than this one," she said, sighing.

She imagined herself back in her own bathroom, turning on the shiny gold taps and running a deep, hot bath with a big squeeze of her mother's smelly and specially imported bath gel. Then she'd turn on the spa jets and lock the door so she could bubble there for hours without interruption.

"Max?" It was Linden again. What was it about him that just wasn't understanding that Max wanted to be left alone?

"Yeah?"

"Would you like a cup of tea?" Linden asked.

That was another thing about this house. There always seemed to be a pot of tea brewing somewhere, as if they spent half their time drinking the stuff.

"All I need right now is a shower, thank you," said Max, trying to make her voice sound cold so that Linden would go away.

"Okeydokey," sang Linden, before he walked away whistling.

The image of the pristine bathroom in Max's head was gone. There was no spa, no smelly bath gel, just a slab of soap that didn't smell of anything and two ancient taps that screeched like low-flying crows as Max struggled to turn them on.

She sighed and would have given her whole CD collection to be instantly transported off this farm and back home.

When she turned off the taps, she could hear Eleanor, Ben, and Linden down the corridor sharing a good belly laugh.

Great! Farmboy had told them about the mud. Now Ben and Eleanor were going to think she was some klutz from the city, who couldn't even walk straight. Maybe she should just go to her room rather than face the humiliation.

But not before she knew what they were saying about her.

Max tiptoed down the hall to put her ear against the door but as she did, she tripped over a fold in the hall rug and fell forward, crashing through the door and landing face first on the kitchen floor.

"Max, we were waiting for you," smiled Eleanor.

Eleanor, Linden, Ben, and Ralph all beamed down at her.

"Ben has something important he wants to tell us," Eleanor added.

Max got up off the floor and sat down at the table. Why did she always find herself on the ground when big things happened?

Ben stood up and made a show of straightening his shirt. Not that it made any difference—it looked old enough for Moses to have worn it. He picked up a glass and clanged a teaspoon against it.

"Ladies and gentleman, may I have your attention please," he said in a very dramatic voice.

Everyone got quiet.

"And may I have a drumroll too?"

Eleanor and Linden banged their hands on the table drumroll style. Ralph gave a loud howl and, from outside the wire door, Larry chimed in with a few loud snorts.

Max stared at them and wondered why Ben didn't just get to the point.

He leaned down and focused steadily on Linden and Max. "What I am about to reveal to you is the result of years of hard work, a few explosive mistakes, and a belief that it could be done, despite all those who told me that it couldn't." Ben let forth a wide-brimmed smile. "And now that it's ready, I can't think of a more special bunch of people to tell."

Max felt her breath catch in her chest.

Ben straightened up before throwing out his chest and continuing, "This morning, Professor Benjamin J. Williams in his humble yet sturdy laboratory in Mindawarra, Pennsylvania, discovered the key to the secret of matter transportation."

Eleanor and Linden burst into cheers and applause.

"It has a few hiccups," he went on. "But I believe that with a few simple modifications it will be ready to present to the world."

Eleanor jumped up and swung her arms around Ben's neck.

Linden jumped up and swung his arms around Max's neck.

"What the . . . ?" Max pulled away.

"Sorry, I got excited," Linden apologized and put his offending hands in his pockets.

Ben and Eleanor, meanwhile, were in the middle of another long and sloppy kiss. Couldn't they wait until they were alone? *I hope they're not going to be like this all vacation*, thought Max. Puke city! She had to stop them and get them back to the important point.

"Can we see it?" she interrupted.

Ben let Eleanor go.

"Sure. Why don't you and Linden make a few sandwiches to take down to the shed, and I'll show you how it works?"

Max had never made sandwiches quicker in her whole life. Within ten minutes they were all seated, ready for the demonstration.

The shed was like nothing Max had ever seen before. There were large benches packed so full of stuff that you couldn't see the surfaces. There were wires and panels with dials and switches and lights and tubes and transistors and cords and rolls of wire and jars and boxes of all sorts of bits and pieces. There were tools and manuals and newspapers and flashlights and tea cups and soldering irons and protective goggles and a miniature replica of Big Ben. The walls were plastered with maps and diagrams and rough sketches of plans, machines and ideas and hats and a few crumpled lab coats, and, of course, there were the millions of books that seemed to be in every room of Ben and Eleanor's house. But tucked away in a corner, only just visible in all the clutter of the shed, Max saw a small shelf with a snow dome of London and a small photo frame with a young-looking Ben and another man he had his arm around, both smiling at the camera.

Max would never have guessed from the outside that this is what she would find in Ben's shed.

Ben stood next to a workbench, where a small object was hidden underneath a cloth.

"And now for the moment we've all been waiting for," he announced.

Max sat on the edge of her seat, curious to see what was under the cloth.

"But first," said Ben, "I want to say something."

Max's shoulders slumped. Why did he have to drag everything out?

"I want to thank a few people who have been very important in making this happen. First, Linden, who has always been a good friend and whose help around the place has made everything for me and Eleanor so much easier."

Ben and Eleanor clapped and Linden's face went so red you could use it as a torch to see in the dark.

"Next, I want to thank Eleanor, who has always believed in me and stood by me every step of the way." He gave a small, crooked smile. "Even when some of my ideas must have seemed a little kooky."

Ben leaned over and kissed her.

Max groaned. All this mushy stuff was really getting embarrassing.

"And finally, I would like to officially welcome Max. It's been a long time since we've had a visitor, and Eleanor and Linden and I want you to think of this as your home."

All three of them turned toward Max and clapped.

She shifted awkwardly in her chair and was probably red-der than Linden was. She wanted someone to say some-thing to take their attention off her.

"And now for the moment we've been waiting for. Ladies and gentleman, I give you the key to the Matter Transporter."

Ben flung off the cloth and on the bench was a small, purple, boxlike device. At the top end was a small, round, glass knob that looked like a remote sensor and on the front was an LED screen with a grid drawn across it. Below that was a keypanel, like a computer keyboard, but with three extra keys labeled *scan*, *activate*, and *transport*. On the side, a long, thin, pencil-like stick nestled into a plas-tic groove, and in the top right corner was a green bleep-ing light above the word *power*. Ben stood with his chest puffed up with pride and a smile that spread right across to his ears.

"Introducing the Matter Transporter control panel," Ben cried. "Max, come over here and you can have the honor of trying it out."

Max walked over and Ben handed her the peculiar device.

"This light indicates your power supply," said Ben. "When it's green, the control panel is in operation, but when it turns red, you know you are running low on power and need to recharge it. You can either leave it in the sun for a few minutes to fully recharge it, thanks to these ultrapowerful solar cells on the back, or simply plug it into the nearest socket using this fold-out, multi-adaptable plug with retractable cord."

Ben turned the device over and showed Max the line of gray solar cells and small connector cord that he pulled out and that sprang back when he let it go.

"This button at the top is for a microcamera that has two main functions. First, it records images of any place you are in. The image appears on the LED screen. After you have captured the image, you use the plastic rod at the side to draw an outline on the screen around the items you wish to transport, thus defining the limits of the transporter capsule."

Max was intrigued by the power of such a small machine and was doing her best to take in everything Ben was saying.

"The second function of the microcamera is as a scanner. You simply point the camera at any map, atlas, or street directory, and, after pressing the scan key, the control panel will, in just a matter of seconds, record all the contents of the map and absorb it into its vast memory. All you need to do then is, using the rod, type the name of the place you would like to transport your goods to. The control panel will work out the coordinates and, just by pressing the *transport* key, do the transporting."

"What will we transport?" asked Max, eager to see a demonstration.

Ben looked around him.

"This sandwich," he said, picking up a ham and cheese sandwich. "Why don't you create the transporter capsule for us?"

Max's eyes lit up. At home she was barely allowed to turn on the TV without asking her mom first, and here she was being asked to operate a new, scientific invention that could change the world. Holding the plastic rod carefully, she drew an outline around the image of the sandwich displayed on the LED screen.

"Excellent! And now let's bring this baby to life," said Ben, speaking so fast his words ran into one another.

Max held the rod in one hand and the control panel in the other. She took a deep breath and, squinting her eyes, brought the rod slowly onto the *activate* key.

There was a quick *zap* sound and then nothing.

"And there she is!" Ben beamed.

Eleanor, Linden, and Max stared.

Ralph gave a confused yelp.

"Well, what do you think?" asked Ben excitedly.

The three of them didn't know what to say. They looked at each other, wondering who should speak first. Eleanor made the first move.

"There's nothing there," she said softly.

Ben laughed. "Oh, it's there all right, you just can't see it."

He put out his hand to touch the sandwich and there

was another zapping sound and a quick flash of light.

"What was that?" asked Linden, taking the words right out of Max's mouth.

"It's the transporter capsule," explained Ben, wanting to get on with the rest of the demonstration. "An invisible electromagnetic field that is created around any item you want to transport."

Eleanor, Linden, and Max stared in astonishment. Ben grinned wildly.

"Now, let's start with something simple and try to transport the sandwich to another position in this room. How about there?"

He pointed to a wooden box near the door.

Max took the rod and typed in the command. The control panel whirred softly as it processed the coordinates of the box.

Ben's voice quivered as he stood beside her.

"Now press the *transport* button," he said.

Eleanor and Linden threw each other nervous smiles. They'd seen a few of Ben's attempts at creating a matter transporter before, and had watched him sag with disappointment each time it had failed. They crossed their fingers, hoping this time it would be a success.

Max started to think about what she was doing. What if Ben was a complete nut? Or they all ended up somewhere cold like Siberia or the North Pole? Or in hyperspace where no one could ever reach them?

But then Max thought of Alex Crane, Superspy, and knew she'd been in far more dangerous spots and had never let fear stop her from embarking on a new adventure.

"Here goes," she said quietly.

Max pressed the rod onto the key and couldn't believe what happened next.

The shed shook. Smoke stared to rise around the sandwich. There was a whirring sound that got louder, like a plane speeding up for takeoff. Eleanor and Linden held each other's hand. Then there was a huge crash of sound like an explosion and a blinding white light that seemed to last for ages.

Then . . .

There was quiet.

Smoke rose from where the transporter capsule was supposed to be and when it cleared they couldn't believe what they saw. Or didn't see. The sandwich was gone.

It worked! Ben's Matter Transporter really worked!

With a little hitch.

The sandwich had landed on Linden's head.

Ben took the sandwich and examined it. It looked perfect.

"This is one of the hiccups I was talking about. Sometimes what I transport doesn't land exactly where I want it to, but that can be ironed out. Apart from that, we've done it!"

Linden and Eleanor cheered.

Max just stared at the control panel in amazement before slowly lifting her head. She had an idea. This little machine could change the world, but more important, it could be the answer to getting her off the farm and back to civilization.

"Can it transport people?" she asked.

"Whoa. Not so fast," cautioned Ben. "This machine is purely for transporting matter, not people. It'll be years before the technology will be developed to transport humans safely."

"But it could happen? One day?" asked Max eagerly, unable to bear the thought of an entire vacation stuck in hillbilly land.

"You bet! In fact, I know of a scientist living in another part of the world who is working on a machine that will transport people not only through space but through time as well."

Max stared at the small purple object in her hands. Could it be true? Could this little device one day transport people through time and space?

"People have been trying for years to discover the secret of this type of travel and so far no one has managed to conquer it," explained Ben importantly. "And here in Mindawarra, we've gotten a little bit closer. But I must warn you." Ben's voice took on a serious tone. "What you've just seen and heard must stay top secret. There are certain people who would do anything to get their hands on the Matter Transporter, and if they did, the consequences would be unthinkable." His grave voice then lightened. "And now we need to celebrate! Linden, why don't you and Max go and get the okay from your dad to stay overnight, and Eleanor and I will get the party ready."

"All right! A party!" Linden shouted.

When Max and Linden left the shed, Max couldn't stop thinking about the Matter Transporter and the fact that in just a short time, she could be off this farm for good. Even though she was enjoying the idea of going home, thoughts about the mystery scientist kept pestering her.

"Do you know who the scientist is that Ben was talking about?" she asked.

"His brother," said Linden, like it was no big deal.

"His brother?" said Max incredulously.

"Yeah—Francis. Ben doesn't talk about him. They worked together in England but then they had a big fight and Ben and Eleanor left. They haven't spoken since."

"Is he the one with Ben in that photo in the shed?"

"Yep. It's a pretty old photo, though." Linden smiled. "That's back when Ben had more hair."

Max ignored the hair comment.

"Do you think Francis might really be close to creating a Time and Space Machine?"

"Well, Ben reckons he's smart enough to do it, but he

doesn't want to have anything to do with him. I reckon it must have been a really bad fight."

Max's head was full of questions. Why did Ben and his brother fight? Where was Ben's brother now, and was he close to completing the Time and Space Machine? Or was it a far-off dream that only a few weirdo scientists were interested in? And who else was interested in getting their hands on it—and why?

Either way, Max was sure Ben was being overcautious about the Matter Transporter, which she was sure could become the world's first People Transporter.

And she would be its first passenger.

CHAPTER 6

Retro Galaxy Guns and a Lost Brother

Chronicles of Spy Force:

Alex Crane had only minutes to save the world from total destruction. The fiendish Clarissa Latham was going to use her Retro Galaxy Gun to destroy Earth's orbit and send it hurtling into the sun if she wasn't handed all the gold on Earth. Just before the deadline, Clarissa's bungling assistant, Jimmy the Rat, accidentally leaned on the detonator button, and the countdown to the end of life as we know it began.

The only way to stop the countdown was to go back in time to Clarissa's hideout and keep Jimmy from pressing the button.

With the seconds ticking by, Alex set the coordinates on the Matter Transporter control panel, pressed the *transport* button, and was hurled at twice the speed of light into Clarissa's hideout. All she had to do was destroy the Retro Galaxy Gun before Clarissa and Jimmy could have their evil way.

Just get to the gun before Clarissa could . . .

"Max. It's ready," a voice called.

Max closed her book. She would finish writing about Alex later; for now she had her own spy mission to complete.

When Max went to the dining room, she stood in the doorway with her mouth sprung wide open. The table was

61

laid out with fine silver and china and food that stretched from one end to the other. Ben and Eleanor were in their best clothes and even Linden was scrubbed up to look pretty decent.

"You might want to close your mouth. The flies can get pretty bad at this time of year," said Linden, trying to hold back a smile.

Max did as she was told and shot Linden a look that made him realize his humor was as welcome as a bowl of worms.

Ben pulled out a chair for Max.

"Madam, dinner is served," he said in a posh accent.

Max looked at the table and wondered how her arteries would survive. At home they only ever ate salads and low-fat meals that wouldn't cause pimples, increase stress, or make you fat. According to her mother, anyway.

But it had been a long time since Max had eaten and she was so hungry that she could manage anything.

There was lots of excited talk and passing of plates as Max sat at the table and thought about what to choose. Thing was, though, after she'd scraped the sour cream off the potatoes, piled her plate with honeyed carrots, and said no to the pyramid of sausages that came her way, she took her first bite and thought she felt her stomach turn over itself. It was one of the best meals she'd ever tasted and she heard very little of the conversation that filled the kitchen as she took more than she'd usually eat in weeks.

Max's mother called just as they'd finished eating. She sounded like she was at a party. Max was so excited to hear from her that she forgot about their fight and instantly began telling her everything that had happened, but after only a few seconds, her mother cut her off.

"That's lovely, darling, but I have to go." It was hard to hear her over the loud music and laughter. "Work calls. Have fun."

The line went dead.

Max stared at the receiver. There was so much more she'd wanted to say.

She hung the phone up and went back to the kitchen.

Later, when they'd celebrated themselves out, and Linden and Eleanor had gone to bed, Max sat with Ben on the verandah as the rain began to fall on the corrugated-iron roof.

"Here's the rain that Larry predicted," said Ben. "He sure has a good nose, that pig."

It was true! Larry was right. Or it was just a coincidence. Either way, it was raining.

Max looked at Ben, who was staring up at the rainy night sky.

Now was her chance. If she handled it right, here was her opportunity to find out more about the Matter Transporter.

"Ben, what would be the worst thing that could happen if the Matter Transporter was used for humans?"

Ben rubbed his hands across his full belly and sighed.

"It's too early to tell, Max. We have to get it right for transporting objects before we start trying it on humans."

Not happy with that answer, Max tried again.

"But if the sandwich was transported in perfect condition, then maybe the same could happen with people."

Ben smiled.

"I'd love to be able to tell you you're right Max, and maybe you are, but for now I'd say it is better to stay on the side of safety until we work out a few more things."

Max was convinced that Ben was just being overly cautious and she believed that the machine was safe.

As they listened to the rain, Max looked out into the distance. You couldn't see Ben and Eleanor's neighbors from the farm, and the town was even farther. All there was, as far as the eye could see, was blackness. There was a whole world outside this place, thought Max. And Alex Crane spent her time traveling all over it. What if there were a machine that could zap you places in an instant? Max thought about how different her life would be then.

"Ben, how far away are we from inventing the Time and Space Machine?"

He frowned.

"That's a hard thing to estimate, Max. It could be years away or right under our noses."

"And you know the scientist who is working on it?" asked Max.

Ben stopped looking at the black distance and stared at the ground.

"Yeah. We were close. Once."

"What happened?" asked Max.

Ben shifted in his seat and bit his thumbnail.

"We didn't agree on something very important," he said quietly.

"Do you still keep in touch?"

Max could see a kind of sadness creep into Ben's eyes.

"The last we heard he was living in London and working for the government," said Ben, taking a deep breath and looking up again as if he were searching for something.

"Sometimes, Max, people have differences that make them feel they can't speak to each other any more," he said. "It's sad, because he was a great guy and it ate me up that we parted on such bad terms."

Ben let out a long sigh. "It's been a big day, kiddo. Better hit the sack. We've still got lots of work to do if we're going to make the transporter perfect."

He stood up and gave Max a kiss on the top of her head. "It's good to have you here, Max," he said with a smile. "I know Linden loves having you around. Someone his own age, rather than a couple of old fogies like Eleanor and me. 'Night."

Max watched Ben as he walked away, his shoulders heavier than when they had first sat down. All she had wanted to know was whether the transporter was safe enough to get her off this farm, but after all Ben had told her, why did she feel so bad? She'd never had an adult confide in her as he had. It made her feel special, but also sad.

And she hadn't realized that Linden liked her. After she'd been such a jerk to him! She'd never had any real friends. Not for long, anyway. She'd moved so many times because of her parents' jobs that when she met kids she liked, it wasn't long before she had to say good-bye to them. So the easiest thing was not to make any friends at all. Saved on all those good-byes.

She looked in the house and saw Linden asleep in a bed near hers. He was okay. After a little while, he might even grow on her. Maybe being on the farm wasn't such a bad thing after all. In the city, all she'd do is stay at home and listen to music and wait for her mother to get in late and barely notice she was there. Whereas here, Ben, Eleanor, and Linden actually seemed to like her.

She thought about Ben and how he was sad about his brother but wasn't doing anything about seeing him again. Max didn't understand it, especially since they could both be working on the Time and Space Machine together.

Then she had a brilliant idea. It was so brilliant she almost yelled out. She would go. Max would take Ben's Matter Transporter to go to London and find his brother, tell him how Ben felt, and get the two of them talking. She'd also see if he'd finished the Time and Space Machine and if he hadn't, she'd help the brothers change the world with it.

Max stayed on the verandah for what felt like hours thinking about her mission. She imagined how proud of her Alex Crane would be. It was a long while later that she let out a big yawn and realized how tired she was. Tomorrow would be a great day, but now she was worn out and before she traveled anywhere, she needed to get some sleep.

CHAPTER 7

Mission:
Matter Transporter

The next morning after breakfast, Ben asked Linden for help around the farm. Ben handed him a list: clean out feed troughs, feed Larry and Ralph, clip the front hedges. Farm and house stuff that didn't sound too interesting to Max, but Max needed time alone with Linden.

"I'll help," she offered.

Ben and Linden looked at Max as if she'd grown two heads. Ben frowned.

"You sure about that?" he asked. "It's messy work. Especially after last night's rain."

"There's nothing wrong with a little dirt," said Max, trying to look enthusiastic. "Let's go."

Linden felt Max's forehead and turned to Ben.

"Feels okay. No fever or anything."

"Ha-ha, Mr. Smartypants," said Max. "Let's make a move before you kill everyone with your sense of humor."

Eleanor stood up. "I'll get you one of Ben's old shirts to wear. And Linden's got a spare pair of overalls you can have."

Max looked down at her clothes. They were new, and she could just hear her mother if she even as much as looked out the window at dirt.

And then, as if Eleanor had read her thoughts, she said, "Your mother won't be happy if we send you back with all your clothes caked in mud." She smiled and went to get the clothes.

So her mother had always been as picky as she was now, thought Max.

After she was dressed, Max strode into the kitchen, ready for action.

"Okay, Linden, let's go. We've got lots to do and there's no time to waste."

She marched past Ben, Eleanor, and Linden and through the door. Ben shrugged his shoulders, as unable as Linden was to explain where Max's sudden enthusiasm for dirt had come from. Linden grabbed an extra piece of toast and followed her.

The more he knew girls, the less he understood about them. He decided then and there to give up even trying.

Outside, Linden threw the toast to Ralph, who ate it in one gulp. He picked up a shovel and headed over to Larry's trough.

"You can start by bringing those buckets around," he began. "And then . . ."

"There's no time for that," said Max. "I have a proposition for you."

"A proposition?" Linden said, confused. "It's just a feed trough."

"I know what it is. I want to find out if you can help me out with a mission I'm working on."

Linden laughed.

"Are you from some secret spy organization or something?"

"Sort of," said Max.

Linden turned to Ralph.

"It looks like Max. It sounds like Max. But I think aliens must have come and switched bodies with her in the middle of the night."

"If you don't want to be involved, just say so and I'll find someone else."

Linden stared at her.

"There's no one else around for miles."

He had a point.

"Okay, then you'll have to do," said Max, eager to get on with explaining the mission.

But Linden wasn't so easily won over and wanted her to know it.

"Maybe I'm busy and won't have time to help you."

"Busy!" yelled Max. "What are you going to be busy with?"

"Oh, this and that," he said.

Max suddenly realized she was being baited.

"Okay," she said quietly. "I want to work with you."

Linden was impressed. Max really did have emotions.

"Sure, I'll help. What's the mission?" he asked.

"I want to use Ben's Matter Transporter to go to London and find his brother. Then I can tell him how Ben feels about him, and find out how close he is to completing the Time and Space Machine that will make them both famous."

Linden was impressed.

For a second.

Then he just thought Max was crazy.

"But Ben said the Matter Transporter wasn't ready to transport humans," he reminded her. "Who knows what will happen if you try it on yourself?"

"Not just me," smiled Max. "You're coming too."

"Me? Why me?" Linden shouted.

"Well, I can't go on my own. I'll need help. London's a big city and it will take at least two people to find Ben's brother."

"What if we get killed? What if the machine makes zombies of us? What if we end up floating in outer space for the rest of our lives?" said Linden, not sure he liked the idea of being transported across the world in a machine that couldn't properly transport a sandwich across a room.

"If the sandwich was transported in perfect condition, I'm sure we could be as well."

Linden wasn't convinced, so Max tried a different approach.

"And what if we sit here and never try it?" argued Max. "Ben will never meet his brother again, the world may never know about the Time and Space Machine, and we will have passed up an adventure that most top spies only dream about. So, what do you say?"

Linden thought about it. Max sure did have a way with

words, and he'd never had anything as exciting as this offered to him in his life. Just farm jobs and the odd trip to the city.

"When do you want to go?" he asked.

"Tonight," said Max.

"Tonight?"

"When Ben and Eleanor are in bed. Hopefully that will give us enough time to find Francis, tell him about Ben, and get back here before they even notice we're gone. If it does take longer, we can leave a note saying you've taken me fishing or whatever it is you do in the country, and we'll be home later."

"You don't muck around, do you? Are you always like this when you want something?" asked Linden.

"Always," said Max with a smile. "Are you in?"

Linden thought about what he was being asked to do. There was something about Max's excitement that got to him and now he didn't want to miss being part of the mission.

"Sure."

"Great!" said Max. "You tell your dad you are staying here again tonight, which Ben and Eleanor won't mind. I'll set my watch alarm for two A.M. and we'll sneak out to the shed and leave soon after that, which means we'll be in London at about seven-thirty A.M. Here," she said, handing Linden a scrap of paper. "I've drawn up a list of some essentials to pack."

Linden looked over the list. Backpack, flashlight, penknife, money, ID, string, handkerchief, notebook and pen, warm clothes, raincoat, watch, and energy bars.

"So, I'll see you tonight?" asked Max.

"Sure," said Linden, thinking about what was ahead of them.

"Let's shake on it," said Max.

Linden offered his hand.

"No," she said. "The secret spy shake."

Max touched her nose and ran her hand through her hair.

Linden stared.

"That's it?"

"That's it. The secret shake of spies. Much less obvious than a handshake and being discreet is the name of the game."

Linden held out his hand slowly, unsure of this new rule, and did the shake. "I'll see you later. There are a few more things I need to do before our mission begins."

"Eight o'clock tonight, and wear something warm. It's cold at night over there this time of year."

Max walked away feeling excited and a bit scared. Part one of the preparations for Mission Matter Transporter was complete. All she needed now was to put the final details in place, and for that she needed Eleanor.

Max went back to the house just as Eleanor was getting ready to go out.

"Eleanor, can I ask you a few questions?" Max asked.

Eleanor was happy to see that Max was feeling more at home and put down her bag.

"Sure. What would you like to know?"

"You and Ben once lived in England, didn't you?" asked Max.

"For four years," Eleanor explained. "That's where we met."

"And why did you leave?"

Eleanor grew quiet.

"It's a long time ago now. Ben and I were working on a secret project for the government when we found out that not everything we were told was true, and in some cases, was an outright lie."

"And you left?" Max asked.

"Yep. We decided we needed a big change and moved here."

"What about Ben's brother?"

"Ah, you know about Francis?" Eleanor said softly.

"Ben told me. But he didn't say too much," Max added.

"He never does." Eleanor smiled. "Come with me, I want to show you something."

Max followed Eleanor to a room at the front of the house. She was amazed when Eleanor opened the door and showed her in. There were computers, boxes, and books everywhere. She'd never even known this room existed.

"This is my study. I don't let too many people in here, mainly because it's such a mess. In fact, you're the first person other than me to step through these doors in a long while. Now, where is that book?"

Eleanor searched the shelves as Max stared at the walls. All around them were framed degrees, certificates, and awards with Eleanor's and Ben's names on them.

"Ah, here it is. You're also the first person in a long time to see what I'm about to show you."

She took a large, important-looking book from the top shelf. She blew across the top and an avalanche of dust flowed across the room.

"It's longer than I thought," she scowled. "This is a scrapbook of our time in England. Ben and Francis were very accomplished scientists, and famous throughout the scientific world for their work."

Max looked carefully through the book, which was full of even more certificates and awards and a letter from the prime minister telling them what a great service they were doing for the world. There were newspaper and magazine articles praising their work, and photographs of them accepting awards and shaking each other's hand with big grins on their faces.

"They look really close," Max observed.

"They were," Eleanor said. "That's why it's so hard for Ben to talk about it now."

"What happened?"

"When we discovered we weren't being told the truth, we were furious and decided to leave. It was a matter of principle. But Francis thought we were overreacting. He and Ben had a big fight about it, and they haven't spoken since."

"That must have been sad," said Max.

"It was. For all of us. We were so close and then it ended. It's hard saying good-bye to friends."

Max thought of the times in her life she'd had to say good-bye, and how each time it hurt as much as the last.

"We often think about Francis and wonder how he is," said Eleanor, staring at the photographs.

Max looked at Eleanor and felt close to her.

"Can I keep looking through this?" asked Max, holding the book.

"Sure. I have to go into town for a few things but you're welcome to stay in here as long as you like."

Eleanor turned to go out.

"And I'll close the door so you can have a bit of privacy."

There was a study in Max's home but she was never allowed to use it in case she made a mess of her mother's things. Living with Eleanor and Ben was really different from living at home.

"Eleanor!" Max said.

Eleanor stopped at the door.

"Yes?"

Max was grateful to her aunt for all she'd done. The

way she treated her, telling her all those private things, everything, but all she could think to say was, "Thanks."

"You're welcome."

Eleanor closed the door quietly behind her.

Max sank deeper into her chair and slowly turned the pages of the book. Eleanor wasn't kidding. The two brothers really were famous. The newspaper clippings were filled with praise for all their work:

"Science Brothers Head Top Secret Project."

"Brothers Search for Key to Time."

"Brothers Set to Change the World."

Max came across an interview with the head of the government department that Ben, Francis, and Eleanor were working for. Her first big lead. She wrote down the name, the Department of Science and New Technologies, and the person in charge, Professor Valerie Liebstrom. But it wasn't until she came across a letter from London that she knew she'd hit the jackpot.

It was addressed to Ben and Eleanor and was from Professor F. J. Williams.

Bingo! Ben's brother. It was postmarked a few years ago, but he might still be at the same address, or, if not, maybe someone there would know where he lived.

Max wrote down the address, closed the scrapbook, and put it carefully back in its place. She then searched for a telephone directory of London so she could scan it into the control panel. She looked through the shelves of books and, tucked between a travel guide to Africa and a book called *The Complete History of Elves*, she found one. The London phone book. It was dog-eared and wrinkled, with food stains smudged across it and sticky tape plastered all over it to keep it together, but more importantly, it had maps of all London's streets. Max tucked it beneath her shirt and thought Eleanor wouldn't miss it if she took it with her. All she needed now was to use it to transport Linden and herself to London, where, by this time tomorrow, she hoped to have met Ben's brother, Professor F. J. Williams, and his Time and Space Machine.

CHAPTER 8

Fried Monkey Brains
and a Secret Pact

Chronicles of Spy Force:

Dr. Harschtorm smiled as he pulled the lever that lowered Alex Crane toward a pit of writhing, slithering snakes.

"They haven't eaten for weeks and are ready for a grand feast," he said. "And you, my dear, are the main course."

Alex had to think, and fast!

There were only minutes to go before the snakes would eat her alive. Harschtorm sat back, ready for the show, as he ate his own specially prepared banquet. Fried monkey brains cooked within the monkey heads. His favorite.

"Bon appetit, my little ones," Harschtorm laughed.

Alex thought if only she could reach into her backpack and get out her Hypno Ray Gun, she could blast Harschtorm and his goons, hypnotizing them into raising the lever and letting her go, but not before she dropped her Destructo Pellet, a small pill that would destroy Harschtorm's headquarters in seconds. But what would become of her?

Just reach a little farther . . .

⊕

"Hi."

Max jumped in fright and turned to see Linden chewing on a carrot.

"Don't sneak up on me like that," Max cried. "You scared me!"

With her heart still pounding from Linden's sudden appearance, she put her book back in her backpack.

"I had something to eat." Linden finished the carrot.

"What were you writing?"

"Nothing. Just scribbling." Max blushed. She'd woken before the alarm and had started writing about Alex to calm her nerves.

Linden was skeptical.

"Looks pretty involved for just scribble."

"All right," said Max, knowing Linden wasn't going to let it go. "But you have to promise not to tell anyone."

"Sure," Linden smiled. "I'm good at keeping secrets."

"I'm writing about Spy Force, the super intelligent spy agency that's been set up to capture criminals all around the world, and Alex Crane is their top spy."

Linden laughed and Max was instantly sorry she had told him.

"That's great. I love spy stories," cried Linden.

Max was wary.

"Do you really?" she asked.

"I know each James Bond story by heart, have watched every *Get Smart* episode ever made, my favorite movie and series is *Mission Impossible*, and my dad and I often sit down to watch his video collection of *The Man from U. N. C. L. E.*"

"You really know your stuff." Max was impressed.

"Can I read some of Alex Crane?" asked Linden.

Max had never shown her stories to anyone.

"Maybe. Someday. But now we have to prepare for departure."

"Whatever you say, chief." Linden saluted.

"Max will do."

Linden was wearing a big, floppy, hand-knitted sweater and what Max thought was probably his best pair of jeans. Well, at least they weren't full of patches or splattered with mud.

"Have you got the note?"

Linden handed Max a piece of paper.

"Max and I have gone expoloring," she read. "I think she needs me to teach her the beauty of the country. Be home by lunch."

Max looked up. "The beauty of the country?"

"It's never too late to learn," Linden answered as if he were an old school professor.

"I'll leave the learning until later. Now we better go."

Inside the shed, the Matter Transporter control panel quietly whirred beneath its cover. Max took the cover off and held the panel in her hands.

"Are you sure you remember how it works?" asked Linden.

"There's nothing to it," Max replied confidently, but secretly she hoped she remembered all the steps.

Max took the London phone book from her backpack and laid it on the bench in front if her. She held the control panel so the camera faced it, and pressed the *scan* key.

There was a small bleep before the LED screen lit up with the words *scan complete*.

Max and Linden looked at each other and smiled.

"That seemed to work," said Linden, relieved that the first part of the process appeared to have gone well.

Max then turned the camera toward them both and captured an image of herself and Linden. Turning the control panel toward her, she saw their image on the LED screen. She used the rod to draw an outline around them both.

"Go easy," said Linden, feigning a concerned look. "Don't cut off any of my hair."

Max frowned, trying to make Linden understand that this wasn't the best time for jokes. She took a deep breath as she held the rod above the *activate* key.

"Here goes," she said as she brought the rod down.

There was the quick *zap* sound and then nothing.

Max and Linden looked around them.

"Did it work?" Linden asked, referring to the transporter capsule.

"I'm not sure. Let's put our hands out and feel around," suggested Max.

They slowly raised their hands until they were met with a flash of light and another *zap* sound. A slight tingling sensation spread through their bodies like a wave.

"Found it," said Linden proudly.

"It worked!" Max almost screamed. "Now to set the coordinates for London."

She adjusted them for Cricklebury Lane, London W6. The home of Professor F. J. Williams.

Max knew she was about to do the scariest thing she'd ever done in her life. She was excited, but she'd also never been as nervous.

"I guess it's time," she said softly.

"We should make a pact," Linden decided.

"A what?" Max asked.

"A pact. Like a deal," he explained.

"I know what a pact is, but we don't have time," said Max, eager to get the mission started and avoid any emotional stuff.

"I'm not going until we do it," said Linden, folding his arms across his chest.

The way Linden said it, Max knew she had no choice. Besides, the sooner she let him get on with it, the sooner they could leave.

"Okay. What's your pact?"

"Hold out your hands," Linden instructed.

Max held out her arms. A zapping sound rang out around as they broke through the transporter capsule's electromagnetic field. Linden took Max's hands in his and closed his eyes as small sparks flew all around them like fireflies.

Max shook her head. This was not the kind of departure she had in mind.

"If Max should come to harm or get lost or be in danger in any way, I, Linden M. Franklin, will do everything I can to help her and bring her to safety."

They both stood in silence.

Linden leaned forward and whispered, "You're supposed to say it about me now."

Great! Just what Max wanted, another mushy moment.

"If Linden should come to harm or get lost or be in danger in any way, I, Max Remy . . ."

She forgot what came next.

"Will do everything I can . . ." Linden whispered.

"Will do everything I can," Max repeated, then frowned, trying to remember the next part.

"To help him and bring him to safety," Linden added.

"Oh yeah, to help him and bring him to safety."

Linden smiled. "Good. Now we can go. All aboard. Express Transporter to London leaving in ten seconds," he announced.

Max looked at her wrist.

"We should synchronize our watches. We will only have about ten hours to complete the mission once we're in London if we're going to get home before Ben and Eleanor wake up. Did you wear your watch?"

"Yep."

Linden pulled up the sleeve of his sweater to reveal a large silver watch that looked like it had been around a long time.

"Are you sure that's going to work?" Max asked.

"It's my granddad's. He left it to me. I don't use it much, but he said it never lost a second."

After they'd checked the time, Max held the control panel in front of her. She wiped her sweaty hands against her pants and adjusted her backpack.

"Here goes," she said.

This was it! If the Matter Transporter worked, in a few minutes they would be in London. But if it didn't, who knows where they'd end up.

Max took a deep breath and carefully placed the rod on the *transport* button.

The shed shook, the transporter capsule surrounding them started to smoke, and a loud whirring sound filled their ears, just like the sound they'd heard when they had transported the sandwich. Max and Linden held their breath as the crash of sound and light exploded around them.

Then . . .

There was quiet.

Smoke rose from where the transporter capsule was supposed to be.

Linden and Max were moving, and fast!

Ralph heard the noise from the yard and crept into the shed. He whined when he saw it was empty.

CHAPTER 9

Slimed!

When Max opened her eyes, she couldn't see a thing. She shook her head but still she couldn't see. When she went to move her arms, she found that they were pasted to her sides but after wriggling them free, she held them up and saw that they were covered in . . . rotten meat!

Yuck!

And the smell!

Where was she? What had happened?

She thought hard. The Matter Transporter. Ben's brother. Time and Space Machine.

She looked around and saw that she was up to her neck in baked beans, moldy fruit, scrapings of old spaghetti, fish, and boiled cabbage.

She'd landed in a giant trash bin!

Great!

She wiped what was left of a piece of custard pie from her head, and felt her body to see if she was okay. Arms, back, legs. Everything seemed fine and the control panel, even though it was covered in tomato sauce and soggy pieces of spinach, was still with her and bleeping happily.

She looked over the side of the bin, and even though it was early, she saw people everywhere. There were street vendors setting up flower stalls, business people in suits rushing across streets and just missing being hit by honking cars, and police walking around in big funny hats. The roads were filling with red double-decker buses, old black taxicabs, and cyclists with courier bags on their backs dodging in and out of traffic. And on either side of the sidewalks, there were picture windows displaying slices of pizza; shops with shoes, clothes, and TV screens playing the same images on each; stands with postcards; shelves of miniature towers and castles; and racks of hats and T-shirts with the British flag plastered all over them.

They'd made it! They were in London! A little soggy, but in one piece and alive! And when she checked her watch, which had also survived the gross landing, they'd arrived in a matter of minutes.

But then she realized that something was missing.

Linden!

Where was Linden?

He must be in the bin! Buried underneath all the slime!

"Linden!" she screamed.

Max searched frantically, pulling up lumps of beef stew, wading through stale pools of soup and dessert glop, picking through half-eaten turkey sandwiches, and still she couldn't find him.

What if something had happened to him? How would she explain it to Ben and Eleanor? And Linden's father? Maybe this had been a bad idea after all.

He could be anywhere. Literally. Maybe he really did end up in outer space, or in another country, or . . .

Max started to panic.

"What am I going to do?" she said out loud. "Linden and I could have been friends. He was a nice guy and the pact we made, even though it was a little corny, was one of the nicest things anyone has ever said to me." Max's eyes became teary. "And I would have done anything to save him if he was in danger. But now . . ."

"Hi."

Max knew that voice.

She turned around and saw Linden eating a large apple and frowning.

"They don't taste any different from the ones at home."

Max stared at him and tried to control her voice. He looked warm and dry in his jeans and sweatshirt.

"Where have you been?" she asked.

"I arrived in the hotel across the street and the guy at the desk gave me this apple on the way out," said Linden, smiling.

"The hotel across the street," Max said with a shiver, as she started to feel the soggy garbage soak through to her skin.

"Yeah. Lucky, huh?"

Linden stared at Max, as if he only just realized where she was.

"What are you doing in that bin?"

"Oh, just waiting for you."

"Looks to me like you were slimed by one of the Matter Transporter's 'hiccups,' " laughed Linden.

Max was trying really hard not to lose her temper.

"Just get me out of here," she said slowly, feeling like a sizzling firecracker before it explodes.

Linden helped Max out of the bin as it started to rain.

"Great! That's all I need," she said, looking up at the gray sky.

"At least this way you won't have to have a shower," Linden joked.

The look on Max's face told him he should cool it with the jokes if he wanted to reach his next birthday.

They ran to a public toilet in a small park nearby, dodging through streams of people who frowned at them as they rushed past. Linden waited outside the ladies room with his hands across his chest to keep warm, and tried to avoid the drips spilling from the small sheltered alcove above him.

Max came out of the ladies room in a much better mood now that she had on clean pants and a shirt from her backpack.

"Okay, we're ready to begin the mission."

Max pulled out her notebook and checked the address. The bin she had landed in was right next to the building where Francis lived. Cricklebury Lane, London W6.

"That's the place, just over there," she said, pointing to the building.

They made a dash across the park and came to the front door of what they hoped was Francis's home. There was a security system with a code to enter the building, which meant that Max and Linden had to wait for someone to go in or out before they could sneak in the door before it closed.

They didn't have to wait long. An old lady dressed in

a long fur coat and holding an even furrier dog walked out.

"Come on, Poochikins. It's time for your morning walk, and after that you're off to the hairdresser for a shampoo and trim."

When Poochikins and the fur lady left, Max and Linden raced forward and caught the door just before it closed. Linden held it open for Max.

"I'm not helpless. I can do it myself, you know," she said.

Linden looked hurt.

"I didn't say you were helpless. I was just opening the door for you."

"Well, you don't need to. We've got a case to solve," said Max as she walked into the building.

Linden stared after her and sighed.

Max walked to the elevator as Linden stopped and looked around the foyer. He'd never been in such an expensive-looking place.

"You'd have to be really loaded if you wanted to live here," he said.

The elevator doors opened and Max stepped in.

"Come on, let's go," she interrupted Linden's inspection of the foyer.

On level nine they found apartment 907. Francis's apartment.

Just as Max was about to knock, Linden stopped her.

"What are you going to say to him?" he asked.

"I don't know. I haven't thought about it yet," Max replied.

"Shouldn't we have a plan?"

"Do you have one?"

He didn't.

"Just knock and we'll take it from there," he suggested.

Max swallowed hard and knocked.

They could hear the sound of a chair being moved and footsteps walking heavily across the floor. They both took a deep breath.

The door opened a crack and was stopped by a chain. A pair of beady eyes above a whiskered chin looked down at Max and Linden.

"What do you want?" the man grumbled.

Max was hoping this grisly old man wasn't Francis.

"We're, um, looking for our uncle," Max stammered. "He lives in this building."

It was obvious the whiskered man didn't like people knocking on his door.

"What's his name then?" he said angrily.

"Francis Williams."

The man's eyes opened wide in fright.

"Never heard of him," he snapped, and slammed the door shut.

Linden looked at Max.

"I guess we said something he didn't like. Let's try one of the others."

Max knocked on the door of apartment 911.

An old lady opened the door and smiled at them.

"Hello there, what can I do for you?"

"Hello," Max said in her best and most polite voice. "We're sorry to disturb you so early, but we were wondering if you wouldn't mind helping us."

"I'd be delighted. What can I do for you? Are you selling cookies or something?"

"No, we're looking for our uncle. He lives in this building but we're not sure which apartment."

"I've lived here for twenty-five years," the old lady said proudly. "If anyone knows your uncle it would be me. What's his name?"

"Francis Williams," said Linden.

You would have thought Max and Linden had set a python loose in her apartment, the way the old lady's face twisted up with fear.

"I don't know him," she said, her voice suddenly icy.

She began to close the door but Max put her foot in the way to stop it.

"Please. You've got to help us. We're from Pennsylvania and it's very important for us to find him."

The old lady looked up and down the corridor to make sure no one was listening. "Your uncle got himself into some terrible trouble," she whispered. "And one day some men in suits came and took him away."

"Why would they do that?" asked Linden, frowning.

A door nearby opened and a man in a suit walked out. He nodded at the old lady and stepped into the elevator. The old lady looked nervous and when the elevator doors were closed she said quickly, "All I know is that one day he lived here and the next day he didn't. I can't tell you any more. Now, please go away."

The old lady closed her door and the sound of ten locks being set echoed around the empty corridor. It was obvious she knew more than she was saying. Finding Francis wasn't going to be as easy as Max thought, but she wasn't going to stop until she had done it.

She turned to Linden.

"Something spooked the old lady and the whiskered man when they heard Francis's name, and we have to find out what and why."

"How are we going to do that if they won't talk to us?" asked Linden.

"We're going to visit the government office where Francis works. And even though I've got a feeling we won't find him there either, maybe we can find someone who isn't afraid to talk."

As Max and Linden waited for the elevator, they heard a noise. Just as they were about to leave, they saw a door to one of the apartments open a fraction, and two spectacled eyes peered out, watching them. Then the elevator doors closed behind them and they were gone.

CHAPTER 10

The Mysterious Man at the Top of the Stairs

As Max and Linden left the building on Cricklebury Lane, Max took out her notebook and scribbled a few lines.

"This is what we've got so far. Francis did live in that apartment but was taken away by men in suits in a sudden and very suspicious departure that the neighbors are too afraid to talk about. We need to find out what has made them so scared. Who were the men in suits? Where did they take him and why? And finally, where is he now?"

Linden took a mint from his pocket and started sucking it. He had a theory.

"My guess is whatever is going on, it's big and involves some very important people. It may even go all the way to the top."

He felt like a spy from a 007 film.

Max was impressed.

"I think you're right," she said.

"Thanks," said Linden. "Want one?"

Linden offered Max a mint.

"Thanks."

The Department of Science and New Technologies was a tall, marble building with statues and carvings of great scientists throughout history in the walls.

As Max and Linden stood in front of it, they felt as if they were somewhere very important. Max patted down her hair and straightened her jacket.

"If people are scared to talk, we have to be careful how we handle this and we have to look and act respectable, so don't do anything that will attract attention."

Max watched Linden try to control his wild curls.

"Well try and look as respectable as you can," she sighed.

"Whatever you say, boss," said Linden.

"And don't call me boss," Max snapped.

"Right, boss," said Linden, trying not to smile.

Max shot him a quick look and walked up the long stairs of the building. She pushed through the heavy revolving door into the foyer and stood on the polished marble floor. Linden walked in and stood next to her.

"Wow! This is some classy building," he said.

Linden had hardly been out of Mindawarra in all his life, and being in London with all its old buildings and statues was like being in another world.

The front foyer was full of paintings, big carpets, and shiny brass everywhere, from door handles to railings to flashy name plates on long polished desks. There were people in suits hurrying all around them, like they were all late for important meetings. Two of them nearly trampled Max and Linden as they stared at the high, superwhite ceilings that were covered in great dangling chandeliers.

In the center of the foyer was a man with a small headset on a glued-to-perfection hairstyle and a smile that seemed to have been permanently affixed to his face. He was sitting at a solid, round marble desk, frantically answering phones, redirecting calls, and saying, "Have a nice day," more often than your average human could have managed in a year. When there was a break in answering phones, Max spoke up.

"Excuse me, we were wondering . . ."

"Good morning, how can I help you?" he asked sharply.

"We're looking for a Professor Valerie Liebstrom," Max said.

The receptionist's smile disappeared instantly.

"Who?" he asked, not sure he'd heard right.

"Professor Valerie Liebstrom," Max said a little shakily.

"That's what I thought you said," said the receptionist in a clipped voice, with one eyebrow climbing high up his forehead to show how annoyed he was at her question.

The man looked around him, then leaned forward, his voice changing from "How can I help you?" to "My day is off to a bad start and you two are only making it worse."

"Listen, kids, Ms. Liebstrom hasn't worked here for quite some time, and if you want to stay out of trouble, you'll have nothing to do with her."

The man answered a few more calls and was irritated to look down and see Max and Linden still standing there.

They weren't taking no for an answer and Max wanted him to get that through to him.

"Look, mister, I've had a really bad morning myself so if you don't want me to scream at the top of my lungs until I break every one of those expensive-looking chandeliers, then you'll hand over the information I'm looking for."

Linden leaned over the desk.

"I'd do it if I were you. She's won competitions back home for this sort of thing."

"Surely you can't be serious," the receptionist sneered. "Now get out of here before I call security."

Max folded her arms.

"I'll give you five seconds. Linden?"

Linden started counting.

"This isn't going to be pretty," he warned. "Five, four, three . . ."

The receptionist was getting worried. These two kids were starting to attract a lot of attention.

"Two . . ."

All around them, people in suits stopped to stare.

"One!"

Max started screaming. A loud, ear-crushing, eye-popping scream. People in the foyer covered their ears. Chandeliers started trembling and clinking overhead.

One of the chandeliers burst into a million pieces, bouncing off the marble floor and sending the suits running everywhere. The receptionist couldn't take it any more.

"Okay! Okay! Make her stop. I'll give you what you want."

Max stopped screaming.

The receptionist took a handkerchief from his pocket,

wiped his brow, and wrote on a piece of paper.

"Last I heard, she could be found at this address, but don't tell anyone I told you."

Max took the paper and shook the receptionist's shaking, sweaty hand.

"Thank you for your help," said Max in her best sugary voice. "And have a nice day." She smiled.

As Max and Linden walked out of the building, stepping over the crouching suits who were still holding their ears, a man in a long jacket stood at the top of the stairs and watched them go. He was surrounded by other men who were bigger than him, wore dark glasses, and looked like they'd never smiled in their whole lives.

The man in the long jacket turned to one of the men and whispered, "Follow them and find out who they are and what they're up to."

CHAPTER 11

Laser Tunnels on the Way to a Nightmare

Outside the Department of Science and New Technologies, Max beamed as she held out the piece of paper the receptionist had given her.

"This is our next vital clue to finding Francis and the Time and Space Machine. Are we good or what?" she cried.

"That was awesome. Spies who'd been in the business for twenty years couldn't have done better than you," Linden cried.

Max smiled and shrugged her shoulders.

"Yeah. I guess it was pretty good."

"Are you kidding? You were great!" shouted Linden.

Max wasn't used to receiving compliments, and her face turned bright red. She took out her notebook and started to write down their new findings to hide her embarrassment.

"Let's just go and find the professor," she said.

Linden realized his praise was maybe a bit much, and his face went red too.

And he hated getting embarrassed.

"Good idea," he said, looking away, but as he did, he thought he saw someone disappear behind a building.

"Max, I don't know what it is, but I've got this feeling we're being watched."

Max turned around.

"Linden, I read in Eleanor's guidebook that there are more than nine million people in this city. Why would they be watching us?" she asked.

"Well, so far, in the short time we've been in London, we've managed to spook the people in Francis's building and freak out the receptionist in the Department of Science and New Technologies. And when we were leaving there, I got the feeling that someone was looking at us."

"You really have seen too many spy films," said Max. "We've got the perfect cover. We're kids. Why would anyone think we were up to anything funny?"

"I guess you're right," Linden said, not really convinced. But he told himself that Max knew what she was talking about. They were just kids. The perfect cover, like she said.

Max looked down at the address that the receptionist had given her: Hartfield School, Salisbury Road, Bleechgrove E7.

"This must be where she works."

Linden frowned.

"But she used to be the head of an important government department. What would she be doing working at a school?"

Max took the London telephone directory from her backpack as they made their way to the nearest Underground station.

"I don't know, but we're about to find out."

Chronicles of Spy Force:

Alex Crane clung to the roof of the high-speed luxury train and adjusted the earpiece of her Micro Descrambler Watch, listening for what was coming next. Inside was the brilliant Madame Des Arbres, the self-made billionairess who owned the largest multinational botanical company in the world and was in the middle of a very secret, high-level meeting with her henchmen regarding the final stages of another evil plan.

Spy Force had uncovered Des Arbres's secret scheme to unleash into the world's forests a virus that would stop trees everywhere from being able to reproduce. Whole countries would be forced to buy her seeds in order to plant more trees, ruining whole economies and making her the richest person in the world.

Alex adjusted the frequency of the Descrambler, which could translate any language in the world, and listened as Des Arbres's French became fluent English.

"If countries don't buy my seeds, whole ecosystems will collapse and they will have no one to blame but themselves."

Alex heard the squeal of arrogant laughter from Des Arbres, as her final detail of dastardly planning was about to be put into place.

"It will not be long now," the Descrambler translated for Alex. "Everything is in order. All we have to do is send the planes to all the major forestry sites of the world and spray our lethal Des Arbres Mist all over them to make them mine."

115

Des Arbres launched into another annoying cackle as Alex switched off the Descrambler and put it into her backpack. The wind rushed by her like a cyclone as she made her way carefully along the roof of the speeding silver train, clinging to every protrusion and handle she could find as she made her way to Des Arbres's carriage. She had with her Spy Force's newest invention, the Neuro Reversal Spectron. With one zap of this powerful device, she could reverse the thinking patterns of all who came under its sphere of influence. All she needed to do was reach Des Arbres's window, aim the Neuro Reversal Spectron at her and her buffoons, and the world's forests not only would be saved but also would have Des Arbres as their most devoted greenie, dedicating the rest of her life to saving the trees.

But just then, Alex's foot slipped. She lost her foothold and dangled from the careening train like a leaf in autumn. She tried to regain her foothold but the force of the wind pinned her against the train so that she was unable to move. As she looked around for a something to hold on to, she saw the narrow mouth of a tunnel ahead, hurtling toward her like a hungry giant. She had about ten seconds to avoid certain doom. Would this be the end of Alex Crane? Would she be able to regain her foothold and avoid her fast-approaching demise? Would the world's forests be wiped out by . . .

The train jerked as it came to a screeching halt. Linden toppled against Max and collapsed into her lap like a rag doll. Max looked down at him.

"Comfortable down there, are we?" she asked.

Linden pulled himself up and adjusted himself in his seat.

"Sorry, must be that magnetic personality of yours drawing me in," said Linden, looking away to hide the smirk creeping onto his face.

"You know, if you put as much effort into being clever as being funny, you'd be a genius by now," said Max, hoping to put an end to the conversation.

"Yeah, but I'd be a bored genius," said Linden into his sleeve.

"What did you say?" asked Max.

"I wonder what the holdup is," said Linden, looking around the carriage and pretending to be interested in what had stopped the train.

Max frowned and went back to her notes.

Linden looked at the people around them. They carried on reading their books or staring at the ceiling as if they hadn't even noticed that the train had stopped. Maybe this happened all the time in London and people were used to it.

He turned to Max. She was still scribbling in her notebook.

"So why are you spending your vacation with Ben and Eleanor?" he asked.

Max had been so caught up in their mission that she'd

forgotten the whole story about her father canceling his visit, the explosion of slime at school, and the fight with her mom. After all that had happened in the past few days, that stuff seemed like ages ago.

Thinking about it now made Max's shoulders tense up, and she turned to Linden with a little more force than she had intended.

"What's it matter to you?" she snapped.

Linden was surprised by Max's anger.

"It doesn't matter. I was interested, that's all. You don't have to tell me if you don't want to."

They sat in silence for a few minutes. No one on the train was moving. The only sound that could be heard was the turning of the page of a book or the occasional cough or snore.

Linden stared at the map of the Underground on the car wall, and Max turned her pen over and over in her fingers, sorry that she'd been so mean to Linden when all he did was ask a question.

The funny thing was, when Max thought about it, she did want to talk. She hadn't had a chance to tell anyone how rotten the whole thing had made her feel. How she felt as if no one loved her and everywhere she went she made a fool of herself, and how she never had any real friends because she was always moving, and how lonely that made her feel, and how most of the time, no matter what she did, she felt that life was stacked against her.

"There was no one to look after me at home in New York," Max spoke up.

Linden stopped looking at the map.

"My dad lives in Los Angeles and he was supposed to come back to New York for summer vacation, but he got this important job and couldn't make it."

Max looked down at the pen that she was turning in her fingers.

"We had some really great things planned too," she said sadly.

Linden reached into his pocket for a mint and offered it to her.

"Who do you live with in New York?" he asked.

Max screwed up her face. "Ms. Popularity."

Linden was confused. "Who?"

"My mother," explained Max. "She's the head of publicity for a big television network, and spends most of her time running after famous personalities at dinners and parties and launches of new TV shows. But if you ask me," Max said, "there's not much personality to be found."

Max had been talking really fast and getting excited. She stopped and let out a small laugh.

"She probably finds those people more interesting than me," she said softly.

Linden wasn't sure, but he thought that Max had a tear in her eye.

"If they all had brain transplants maybe," he said.

Max laughed, but what Linden said made her want to cry more. It was nice. She looked away, not wanting him to see her face. Linden put his hand on her shoulder, but she pulled away from him, took a handkerchief out of her backpack, and blew her nose.

"I must be getting a cold," said Max into her tissue.

Max hated crying in front of other people, but she did feel better now that she'd said all that. She knew that not everything she said was exactly fair, but sometimes things her mom did weren't fair either.

The train lurched forward with a jolt as it slowly started up again. The sound of the wheels on the track beneath them resonated throughout the subway car.

"How about your mom?" Max asked, wanting to change the subject. "What's she like?"

Linden looked out the dark window of the train as it rocketed through the Underground tunnel.

"She died two years ago. Cancer," he said quietly.

Max froze. She hadn't known. No one had told her. What do you say to someone whose mother has died?

Linden stuck his hands under his legs as if he suddenly felt really cold.

"It's okay. Dad's great. He's more quiet these days than he was before, but he's a really good dad."

Max shifted in her seat. She'd never been told any-thing so important in her life and she couldn't think of a thing to say. Not one thing.

"I miss her. Especially at nights when it's quiet and I can still hear the sound of her voice saying good night and telling me to dream of great things." Linden smiled. "She always used to say that."

Max stared at Linden as he looked at the lights of the tunnel flash by like shooting lasers.

The train slowed down, and the squeal of brakes echoed around them.

"This is our stop," he said, standing.

Max followed him to the door of the car and stood by him in silence. She wanted to make him feel better just as he'd made her feel better. She remembered the pact they'd made and went to put her hand on his back, but the doors opened and he stepped off the train.

They said nothing all the way to Hartfield School as they walked past streets with boarded-up shops, thick wire fences across dirty storefronts, and flashing neon signs saying FISH AND CHIPS. There was an old, stone church with bars across the stained-glass windows and cracks in the sidewalks where kids had scribbled with chalk to play hopscotch. They passed tall buildings with gray, cement walls and wash hanging on lines from cramped little balconies, and crossed streets at traffic lights where the cars, buses, and trucks were lined up behind each other in an endless stream. Linden had never seen a place so busy in his whole life and wondered if it ever slowed down.

When they reached the school, they stood in front of

the gates with their mouths open. If Valerie did work here, it was a long way from the flashy foyer of the Department of Science and New Technologies.

The school was like your worst nightmare: a concrete and brick tangle of buildings that looked like they'd been there for decades and no one had bothered to care for them. Everything was gray and crumbling, as if it were going to fall down any minute, and the really strange thing was that there wasn't a single tree to be seen. Anywhere.

Linden screwed up his face.

"Kids really go to school in a place like this?"

"I guess they do," she said, checking the address.

Suddenly an old man grabbed them by the shoulders. Max and Linden screamed.

"So you thought you'd get away with it, did you? Sticking your noses in where they're not welcome. Well, I'll fix that," he growled.

Max and Linden filled with fright. Maybe they had been followed. Maybe they'd gone too far. Maybe someone *really* didn't want them to find Francis. The man looked about a hundred years old and had the meanest face they'd ever seen. And from the way he had grabbed their shoulders, it seemed he meant business. There was no turning back now.

CHAPTER 12

A Darkened Corridor
and Men in Dark Suits

Max and Linden struggled under the tight grip of the old man. Whatever it was that he thought they'd done, he was really angry.

"I'm sick of you kids thinking you can do as you please. I'm going to teach you a lesson you'll never forget," he threatened.

What was he talking about? Where was he taking them? Max was scared, and she was furious at being handled like this.

She wasn't going to take any more.

She gave Linden a wink and with a quick turn, sank her teeth into the old man's arm. He let out a scream loud enough to bring down the crumbling school buildings.

Linden followed Max's lead and bit into the man's other arm. His grip loosened and they twisted away, leaving him to nurse his two injured arms.

"Darn kids. When are you going to learn that you're the ones missing out when you skip class?"

Max looked at him.

"We don't go to this school," she said. "We're from Pennsylvania."

The old man looked confused, and Max couldn't help herself.

"Pennsylvania . . . Philadelphia . . . Liberty Bell," she explained.

"I know where it is," the old man said grumpily. "I'm the geography teacher."

He rubbed his sore arms and mumbled, "I guess I made a mistake. Sorry. What are you doing here?"

Linden straightened his sweater.

"We're looking for a friend," he said. "Professor Valerie Liebstrom."

The old man started to laugh.

"That's rich. So you think she's a professor, do you?"

He kept laughing.

Max was losing her patience.

"Can you just tell us where she is?" she said curtly.

"I'd do it if I were you, mister," Linden warned. "Back home, she's known as Jaws."

Max shot Linden a look that told him to stop. Linden tried to cover his smirk but didn't do it very well.

The old man stopped laughing and pointed to one of the buildings.

"She's in there. End of the corridor. Turn right."

As they walked away, they heard the voice of the old man behind them.

"Professor. That's rich. That's really rich."

Max and Linden had to use all their force to open the heavy, creaking door of the building where they were supposed to find Professor Liebstrom. Max turned to Linden.

"Jaws?" she asked.

Linden could see that Max wasn't happy.

"It was a joke," he explained. "That's something funny that people laugh at."

126

"I know what a joke is," Max snapped, looking down at her watch. "We just don't have time for joking."

Linden frowned. When was having a laugh a waste of time? Max was really in need of an injection of humor.

It had been almost eight hours since they had arrived in London. With only four hours left, they needed to work really fast to try and complete their mission.

Inside the building they could hear the muffled echo of kids talking. There was one light flickering overhead and blackened paint peeling off the walls of the corridor like giant strips of licorice.

Linden was spooked.

"And that old man was wondering why kids skip class," he said.

Max squinted through the darkness. She could just make out the shape of a door.

"That must be it." She pointed.

Just then, the loud clanging of a bell swept through the hall. Max and Linden covered their ears as doors burst open and kids came flying at them from everywhere. They fought their way through a sea of faces to the door at the end of the corridor. It was partly open, and a dusty stream of light spilled out of what looked like a science lab.

"Dr. Frankenstein would have felt right at home here," said Linden.

Max frowned.

"Okay, okay. No jokes," Linden said. "But it's not going to be easy."

Max knocked and pushed the door open wider. Inside was a small woman in a long, white coat, walking between lab benches and gathering beakers, test tubes, and Bunsen burners onto a metal cart.

"Excuse me, are you Professor Liebstrom?" she asked.

The woman looked up and smiled.

"No one's called me that in a long time. And who might you be?"

Linden and Max were relieved. This was the first person in London who hadn't freaked out when they asked a question.

"I'm Max and this is Linden. We're from America and we're looking for Francis Williams."

The woman's smile dropped.

Max froze. Maybe the professor would freak out after all, now that she knew who they were looking for. Valerie Liebstrom was their last real lead, and time was running out if they were going to get back to Pennsylvania before Ben and Eleanor woke up. They couldn't blow it now.

Linden knew this too and tried to think of something to convince Valerie that it was okay to talk to them.

"We don't want to get you into any trouble," he began. "Max's uncle is his brother and we're trying . . ."

"You know Ben?" she asked.

Max and Linden were wary.

"Yeah," they both said slowly.

Valerie smiled and a faraway look came into her eyes, as if she were remembering something from a long time ago.

"Ben and Eleanor," she whispered. "How about that?"

Then she snapped out of her reverie and looked worried.

"Has something happened to them?" she asked.

"No, they're fine," Max burst out. "Ben has created a Matter Transporter and knows that Francis has been working on creating a Time and Space Machine. We know that you once worked with the three of them and Ben and Francis had a fight and don't see each other any more. But Ben really misses his brother, so we've come to find him."

Valerie's eyes brightened.

"And you used the Matter Transporter to get here?" she asked excitedly.

"Yeah. It works!" Linden cried. "It's not perfect yet, but Ben's close."

Valerie had that dreamy look in her eyes again.

"So he did it," she said quietly.

Max looked at her watch.

"Yeah, but we don't have long before we have to leave. Can you help us find him?"

"I can try," she said.

"Mom?" asked a voice behind them.

Linden's eyes widened when he turned and saw a girl standing at the door. She looked about eleven, had dark, curly hair and big brown eyes that looked out at him through a pair of pink glasses. He straightened his sweatshirt and walked over to her.

"Hi, I'm Linden."

Max felt a twinge as she watched Linden speak to the girl.

"This is my daughter Ella," smiled Valerie. "And this is Max and Linden from America. They know Ben and Eleanor and have come to London to find Francis."

"America? How cool. I've always wanted to go to America," said Ella.

Linden's smile reached so far up his face it nearly crashed into his ears.

"Yeah, me too."

He blushed as red as raspberry cordial.

"I mean, yeah, it's a really cool place."

Max was going to be sick. Since when did Linden say "cool"?

"We'd better get going," said Valerie, grabbing her bag. "I know where Francis used to live just a few months ago. We can try there and talk on the way."

Walking to the car, Max couldn't help feeling a little weird when she saw Linden and Ella together. Linden was laughing as if Ella were telling the funniest jokes in the world. Valerie had given them all some fruit from her bag, and Linden and Ella were sharing theirs as they walked. Max ate hers in silence.

In the car, Valerie told them the story of how Francis and Ben came to have a falling out.

"Ben and Francis were working on a top-secret project for the government, which was being supervised by me. They were going to make a Time and Space Machine just as Ben told you. They were close too, until Mr. Blue came on the scene."

Max frowned.

"Who's Mr. Blue?" she asked.

"A very suave man the government hired to be in charge of that project and others that Ben and Francis were working on. He was supposed to sell the machine overseas and make sure England was the first country to succeed in creating it because there were other countries working on it too."

Linden leaned forward from the back seat.

"What happened?" he asked.

"It turns out that Mr. Blue didn't have the best interests of the country at heart. He told Ben and Francis that the machine and the money they made from it would be used to help people in England and in other countries less fortunate than ours, but he really wanted the money to go into his own private account and some dubious nuclear projects."

"Not only that," Ella added, "Mr. Blue was making lots of money for himself from selling government secrets all over the world, and was planning to sell the secret of the

Time and Space Machine when it was finished."

"Does he still work for the government?" Linden asked.

"He has one of the highest positions in the country next to the prime minister," Ella explained.

"He is also very clever at covering his tracks," said Valerie. "We've been trying to expose him for years, but he's not only clever at planning evil schemes, but he's also brilliant at hiding any evidence that they exist. But when Ben found out about Mr. Blue's lies, he quit and asked Francis to come with him."

"And Francis didn't go?" Max guessed.

"Francis is a scientist and wanted more than anything to continue working on the Time and Space Machine. He didn't want to believe that Mr. Blue had lied to them and thought Ben was overreacting."

"That was when Ben and Eleanor went to America?" Linden asked.

"They left as soon as they could," Valerie added with sadness in her voice.

"And Francis stayed?" asked Max.

"Not for long. He uncovered more of Mr. Blue's lies and he confronted him. Mr. Blue told Francis that if he refused to work with him, he'd make sure he never worked in the field of science again. Francis was shocked. He thought that what he was doing was good, but instead he was just part of Mr. Blue's terrible plan. By then he was far away from the two people he loved most, Ben and Eleanor."

132

"And that's when he disappeared," Ella added. "Without a word."

"With the help of a few men in suits," said Linden to Max, remembering what the old lady had told them.

Max and Linden felt sad about the story of Francis and Ben's split. Max really wanted to find Francis now, so she could tell him how much Ben and Eleanor wanted to see him.

"And what about you?" Linden asked.

Valerie sighed as if it were really hard for her to tell them.

"Soon after Francis left, I found out everything. I resigned and told Mr. Blue that I was going to tell the whole world about what he was doing, but before I could, he ruined my career and reputation. He had drawn up some scientific results that were full of flawed work, and told the papers and the TV that I was misusing government money and science for my own advantage. He invented a whole lot of evidence against me. He then called me a disgrace to the scientific community and they believed him. After that, no one would listen to anything I had to say."

Ella looked sad as her mom told the story and Linden took her hand. Ella smiled and blinked a tear from her eye.

"I was kicked out of the department," Valerie said, "and stripped of my security clearance. Nobody believed me when I tried to tell the truth. Mr. Blue was very thorough, and the only job I could get was as a lab assistant at Hartfield School."

Max looked at her.

"Well, we believe you, and we're going to make sure that the world knows the truth about Mr. Blue," she said.

Valerie smiled as she parked the car.

"Here we are," she said.

Max and Linden looked out the window and stared in surprise at the scene around them. The street was full of potholes and on either side were gray, crumbling, apartment buildings surrounded by broken brick fences overgrown with weeds and garbage cans overflowing with trash.

"It looks a little more run-down than when I saw it last," said Valerie.

Max and Linden looked at the building she was pointing to. It seemed like a tired old man, worn out with the effort of trying to stand up.

"Let's go in and see if we can find Francis" said Valerie, trying to inject a positive note into her voice.

As they got out of the car, a black BMW pulled up in silence nearby. Behind its heavily tinted windows sat two men wearing dark glasses and black jackets. One of the men whispered into his mobile phone.

"We've found them, boss. It won't be long now until you have what you want."

CHAPTER 13

The Time and Space Retractor Meter

Max stepped into the building where they hoped to find Francis, and she turned around to see Linden holding the door open for Ella.

"Thanks, Linden. That's sweet," Ella said.

Sweet? That's worth throwing up on, thought Max.

Valerie led them to the elevator, but standing in front of it was like standing in front of a giant bear in hibernation. There were no lights working and not a single crank of steel or cables to be heard.

"Looks like we have to hike the five floors on foot," she said.

Max cringed with the thought that Linden would probably offer to carry Ella up.

On the stairs, Linden and Ella were talking quietly.

"When do you have to go back to America?" Ella asked.

"We have to leave in a few hours," said Linden.

Ella was disappointed.

"Can I give you this?"

She handed Linden a small white machine.

"What is it?" he asked.

"It's a communication, tracking, and recording device," Ella said proudly. "Mom made it so she and I can always be in contact with each other. Just press this button here, and a communication signal will go directly to us."

"That's great! Will it work all the way from America?" Linden asked.

"Mom says it could work from the moon. So we can talk to each other every day."

Big deal, thought Max, who was listening to what they were saying.

Linden beamed, and for a second Max thought he was actually going to give Ella a kiss.

She couldn't stand it any more.

"Linden, can I talk to you?" she asked.

Ella knew something was wrong and stepped past Max to walk with her mom.

"Linden, if we're going to find Francis, you're going to have to keep your mind on the job and not go all gaga over some girl."

"I wasn't all gaga. She gave me this," he said, holding out Ella's present. "It's a communication, tracking, and . . ."

"I saw what was happening. You can chase girls when we get back to the farm. For now we've got an important mission to complete, or have you forgotten that?" Max snapped and walked on ahead.

Linden muttered to himself, "Maybe if you were a little less stressed out, we could finish the mission and have a good time."

Max swung around.

"What did you say?" she asked.

"I said it's a shame the elevator isn't working because it's a hard climb," Linden said, smiling.

Max was skeptical, but spun around on her heel and walked on.

On the fifth floor, Valerie found the room she was looking for. The corridor was dark, and there was a strong musty smell, as if no one had bothered to open any windows for years.

"This is it," she said, looking around dubiously at the papers and rubbish littering the floor.

She knocked on the door.

They waited, but heard nothing.

Valerie knocked again and this time they heard the crash of crockery, followed by an angry snarl and mumbled complaining.

"Stupid, half-witted, ridiculous . . ."

Valerie pulled Linden, Ella, and Max behind her.

They jumped as they heard footsteps clumping toward them. Then there was a thump against the door and a gruff voice shouted, "What do you want?"

"Francis? Is that you?" Valerie was shocked. It sounded like Francis, only older and very angry.

The voice yelled back, "Who wants to know?"

"It's Valerie Liebstrom, and I've brought some people to see you."

There was a pause before the angry voice yelled again.

"Well, I don't want to see anybody, so why don't you all just turn around and go back to where you came from?"

A hush settled on the hall, and Max looked at Valerie.

"Maybe if he knows that Ben's my uncle, he'll listen to me," she said.

Max stepped closer to the door.

"Mr. Williams, my name is Max and I've come all the way from America . . ."

Before she could finish, Francis shouted again.

"Are you still there? I thought I told you to go away?"

Valerie put her hand on Max's shoulder.

"Maybe we should leave," she said.

But something in Max got all fired up, and she suddenly lost her patience for this rude man and wanted him to know it. She and Linden had come too far and done too much to find Francis, and now that they were here, she wasn't sure he was even worth it. If this was how their mission were going to end, she was at least going to tell him what she thought.

"Now, you listen here. You may be sick of the world, but there are some people who'd like to talk to you. If it was up to me, I'd have nothing to do with you because you sound like a mean and cranky old man, but Ben and Eleanor do care. But if that's the way you want to treat . . ."

"Ben and Eleanor?" the voice barked, but this time less loudly.

Max and Valerie looked at each other.

"They're my uncle and aunt and I just wanted . . ." Max began.

"Well, why didn't you say that Ben was your uncle

instead of just raving on?" Francis interrupted.

Ella, Linden, Valerie, and Max stared at the door as the hall echoed with the sound of bolts being drawn. They had no idea what to expect and stood back apprehensively, waiting to see what this man looked like. When the final bolt was released, the door opened with a tired creak and the shadow of a man appeared from the darkness of the apartment.

"Well, don't just stand there," he said. "Come in."

They filed in slowly and when Francis flicked on a small lamp, the whole place took on a dim, blurry focus. The apartment was just one small room, which was the kitchen, bedroom, and living room all in one. On the floor near the lamp was a broken tea cup, which Francis stepped over as he lowered himself into a large, dusty-looking lounge chair. There were piles of yellowing newspapers everywhere, and frayed curtains covered the windows. The fireplace was filled with soot and ashes below a mantelpiece strewn with cups, papers, unopened mail, and apple cores. In the corner was a small, unmade bed, strewn with a tangle of blankets and discarded clothes. In the kitchen area, the table was covered with sauce bottles, cups, plates, salt and pepper shakers, and gooey leftovers from breakfast. Dishes were piled up in the sink like a crooked tower about to topple over. There was a small fridge with a broken handle and, next to this, garbage bags sat like obedient pets, waiting to be taken out.

Max and Linden stared with open mouths. They'd never seen such a mess.

"You might as well sit down," offered Francis gruffly.

When Valerie and Ella sat on the loveseat, a small cloud of dust ballooned around them. Linden perched on the armrest next to Ella and sneezed.

"Bless you," she said, smiling up at him.

Max rolled her eyes and moved away from them to sit on a wobbly kitchen chair near Francis. She studied his face as he stared at the floor. In the photos he was young, handsome, and smiling, but in person he was a small, bony man who looked more like a ghost. Everything about him was gray. Gray hair, gray skin, even his eyes were gray. He looked like someone whose hard times had sunk into his skin and stayed there.

Valerie was the most shocked.

"How have you been, Francis?" she asked, trying to make her voice sound calm.

"I've been better," Francis harrumphed.

He kept his head down as he spoke to Max.

"So what did Ben have to say?" he asked softly.

"That he misses you and is sad that you don't talk any more."

Francis kept looking down.

"He said that, did he?"

"He also said that you were close to inventing a Time and Space Machine," said Max.

Francis looked up.

"That's all in the past now," he said sharply.

Linden moved forward on the armrest. "Ben has created a Matter Transporter and that's how Max and I got here."

"He did?" Francis asked, unable to hide his increasing curiosity.

"And we thought you'd like to come back to America and finish the Time and Space Machine with him," said Max.

Francis looked down at his hands.

"I'm finished with science," he said curtly.

Max looked at Valerie. How were they going to convince him to come with them?

"Francis, you love science," Valerie said. "And your brother needs you."

There was a pause before Francis spoke again.

"When we were kids, Ben and I were very poor. Our dad ran out on us when we were young. Some nights we were so cold we slept in the same bed to keep warm. It was on one of those cold nights that Ben and I made a pact that we would always stick together and we would make something of ourselves so that we'd never be poor again."

Francis wrung his hands in front of him as if he were trying to keep them warm.

"Mr. Blue offered us money we'd only ever dreamed of and a chance to save lots of kids from ever having to be cold or hungry. I thought we had it all. We had money, we were helping the world, and we were together. But the money made me blind to what was really going on. When Ben told me the truth about Mr. Blue, I didn't want to believe it. If I did, I'd have to give up everything."

Francis sighed. "I took someone else's word over my own brother's," he said sadly. "That's something you can never forget."

"But Ben *has* forgotten it," Max almost shouted in excitement. "He really wants to see you again."

Francis smiled.

"We were very close to making the machine work."

"Great, let's go," yelled Max, standing up.

"There's only one thing," Francis interrupted. "There's one vital part of the machine we need. The Time and Space Retractor Meter."

Max and Linden frowned.

"When I left the Department of Science and New Technologies, I destroyed all the files and components of the machine except for that."

Francis smiled as if he were savoring his favorite dessert.

"Mr. Blue has been after it for years. He's offered me everything he could think of, but there's nothing that would make me work with him again, ever."

"Where is it?" Max asked.

"It's in a locker at Victoria Station."

Ella and Linden jumped up.

"Let's go and get it," they said.

They all stared at Francis as he made up his mind. Max gulped hard, hoping he'd agree to come with them.

"As long as all the windows in the car are wound down. I get carsick," explained Francis.

"All right!" shouted Ella and Linden.

Francis picked up a crumpled coat that was draped on the back of his lounge chair as the others made their way out to the corridor. He turned to Max, trying to find the courage to ask what was on his mind.

"You're sure Ben wants to see me?" he asked nervously.

"He said it eats him up that you two parted so badly," said Max.

Francis smiled and looked like he was going to cry. Max hated to see people cry. It was just too much emotion for her to bear. She said quickly, "We'd better get going."

Max walked with Francis down the five flights of stairs.

"Aren't you afraid that Mr. Blue is still after you?"

Francis laughed as he pulled his coat around himself against the cold.

"Mr. Blue has long finished thinking about me," he said.

"How can you be sure?" asked Max.

"He spent years having people follow me. He had my every move watched to make sure I didn't tell the world about him and to find out if I was still working on the Time and Space Machine."

"But why didn't you ever go to police about him?"

"When it came down to it, it was just his word against ours, and because he moved in some pretty important circles, people were never going to believe us against him."

Francis ducked his head as he stepped into the car. He looked awkward as he fumbled to fasten his seat belt. Max leaned between the front seats and fastened it for him. He turned and gave her a crooked smile, as if he knew everything was going to be all right. But something bugged Max. After what she'd heard about Mr. Blue, she wasn't sure he was the kind of person who gave up so easily.

CHAPTER 14

Hired Thugs and a Secret Parcel

Chronicles of Spy Force:

Alex Crane wedged herself into the small passageway just outside the entrance of the Galactatron V that was orbiting somewhere between Mars and Jupiter. On either side of her she could hear the conversations of the evil and foul-smelling Blastaroids who were guarding the Galactatron's entrance. One thing Alex had learned about the Blastaroids was that, even though they were known as some of the most evil, cruel, and repulsive henchmen in the Galaxy, they also had a weakness for incessant talking. Once they started talking, they just wouldn't shut up.

Inside the cabin HQ was Captain Clearstink Glump, the mastermind of one of the most dastardly plans to ever face planet Earth. He had decided during a brief visit to the planet that not only did he like Earth, but that it would also look good in the front yard of his home in Galaxy 423 on the far side of Specter 7. All he had to do was knock Earth out of its orbit, much like a marble out of a chalk circle, and he would have his wish. He was in the middle of toasting his certain victory with a tall glass of Viridion Blast, a mixture of ice cream and melted chocolate he had discovered during his Earth visit, as Alex affixed the Orbit Thruster onto her belt. All she needed to do was adjust the settings of the Thruster, which, if she got it right, would eject the evil ship from Earth's galaxy and place a force field around it, preventing it from ever entering again. Once the process had begun, she would have sixty seconds to leave the ship and be picked up by the Spy Force Space Probe, which was circling nearby, or she would be flung from Earth forever.

"Good luck, Crane. We'll be standing by for your pick-up," Spy Force Probe Deck radioed into her earpiece.

"We are just minutes away from being rid of Clearstink forever," replied Alex.

She heard the continual chatter of the foul Blastaroids near her as she entered the final numbers of the code.

"Bye-bye, Clearstink," she whispered. But as she pressed the detonator, a double reverse thrust from the ship's engines forced the Orbit Thruster from her grasp, and she tumbled onto the floor in front of the large, evil-smelling feet of the Blastaroid guards. They hovered over her, laughing and shouting all sorts of unintelligible things as the seconds melted away for her to make her getaway.

What was she to do? How was she to get away from these intergalactic stinkbombs? The Galactatron V was about to be thrown out of Earth's galaxy forever, and she was their newest passenger. Was this the end of Alex Crane? Would she ever get away from the incessant chatter of the Blastaroid baboons? Would she . . .

$$\bigoplus$$

"Ha-ha-ha!"

Max held her pen in the air above her notebook and

tried to block the laughter from her ears. They were in the car on the way to Victoria Station, and Linden and Ella hadn't stopped talking about what they could do when the Time and Space Machine was finished.

"We could go to Alaska or Antarctica or Andalusia."

"Or we could travel back in time to the land of the pharaohs or the dinosaurs or King Arthur and his knights."

Linden rolled his eyes. "It'd make history lessons a lot more interesting."

Ella nodded. "History isn't my favorite subject either."

Then they went on and on, and talked about favorite films, insects they'd collected, and books they'd read while Francis and Valerie talked about old times and how much they'd missed each other.

If this goes on much longer, Max thought, I'm going to be the first eleven-year-old in the world to spontaneously combust from too much mush.

Max looked out the window at the London streets. There were people everywhere—talking, laughing, and having fun. Then she remembered. This vacation was supposed to be with her dad. She suddenly realized that she missed him and her mom.

Max looked around at the others in the car.

How could you be in a small space with four other people and still feel as if you were all alone!

"Here we are," said Valerie with a quiver of excitement

in her voice. "Why don't you all hop out while I park the car, and I'll meet you at platform six below the clock?"

Francis, Linden, Max, and Ella got out of the car, waved to Valerie, and made their way through the afternoon crowd.

Francis looked nervous.

"There are so many people," he said shakily. "Makes me wonder why I live in the city."

Max moved closer to him and took his hand. If Francis had been a hermit for the past few years, seeing so many people all at once was going to be pretty freaky.

Francis looked nervously at her. He clasped her hand tight as he wiped a handkerchief across his brow with the other.

Around them, the busy station was flooded with announcements of late trains, cancellations, and trains about to depart. There were signs for doughnuts, platforms, and advertisements for new perfumes and vacation destinations. But worst of all, there were people everywhere. Ticket inspectors, police, schoolkids, and businesspeople, and they were all in a hurry.

"Make sure we stay close together so we don't lose each other," Francis shouted above the noise.

Ella slipped her hand into Linden's.

"There are more people here than I've seen in my whole life," said Linden as they were jostled in a dark sea of business suits and long coats.

"It has changed since I was here last, but I think the

152

lockers are over there," yelled Francis, as he led the way through the crowd.

"Ouch!" yelled Max.

Francis turned around.

"What happened?" he asked.

"Some big guy in a suit just stepped on my toe,"said Max huffily.

Francis put his hand on Max's shoulder.

"We're nearly there," he said.

Max scowled and thought about what they'd been through in the past few hours. She'd been slimed, had doors slammed in her face, was almost strangled by a crazed geography teacher, and now she was being trampled by a stampede of people who were twice as big as she was.

Max forced her way between two suits in front of her, and found herself with Ella, Linden, and Francis standing in front of a wall of lockers. Francis stared at one locker in particular.

"This is it. Thirty-two. My favorite number."

Max was elbowed in the head by someone rushing to catch a train.

"I know this is an important moment, but can we open the locker before we all get squashed to pulp?" she said, rubbing her head.

"Sure," said Francis taking a chain from around his neck. He fitted the key in the locker and turned it. With no effort at all, the door opened.

Francis removed a small leather pouch and carefully

took out something wrapped in a white cloth.

Ella and Linden looked at each other in excitement.

Max stood on her toes to get a better view.

Francis unwound the cloth to reveal what they'd all been waiting for. The Time and Space Retractor Meter. A small, shiny, chrome disc with what looked like some kind of voltage meter and flashing lights.

Francis beamed in recognition as if he were seeing an old friend for the first time in years.

"This is it. The secret of time and space travel."

Max turned to congratulate Linden and saw him giving Ella a hug. She looked away until she felt Linden tap her on the shoulder.

"We did it, chief! Mission Matter Transporter has been successful."

Max smiled. They had done it. They were good spies after all.

Francis rewrapped the Time and Space Retractor Meter and put it back in the pouch.

"Now let's get to platform six to meet Valerie before we get trampled," he said.

All four of them began to make their way through the crowd, but it seemed as if there were even more people now than when they'd first arrived.

What happened next was so quick that, afterward, Max and Linden had trouble remembering what really had gone on.

Max could hear Francis's voice shouting for her, but she couldn't see him through the crowd.

"Max, where are you?"

"I'm here," she yelled. But it was no good; Francis couldn't hear her above all the noise.

Max began to feel scared. London was a huge city, and she didn't know her way around like in New York. If she were separated from the others, she'd really be stuck.

"Linden! Where are you?" she called.

"I'm over here!" Max heard Linden's voice but she couldn't see him either.

Just then, a fat man in a brown jacket pushed past Max, and she just managed to see the back of Linden's head.

"Wait for me," yelled Max. But with all the noise no one could hear her. She was hemmed in by so many people that all she could see were different coats and jackets moving past.

"Hey! Get off me!" yelled Max, as one coat engulfed her like a net around a fish. "Get off me!"

Then suddenly everything went black and the ground fell away from under her feet. She was moving through the crowd much faster than she had been before, but her feet weren't touching the ground. She was being carried!

She struggled underneath the coat, but was held so tightly that she couldn't move or make a sound. Then she felt herself being dropped onto a seat, and heard the muffled sound of a man yelling out something as though he were in a great hurry.

Max was in a car, and she was being driven away.

Away from the station.

Away from Linden.

Away from the Time and Space Retractor Meter.

Then she realized the horrible truth.

She was being kidnapped!

CHAPTER 15

Mobile
People Movers

Max woke up with a start, and felt sore and tired and confused.

"Where am I?" she said out loud.

She was in a large comfortable bed, with her jacket and clothes folded neatly at her feet. She looked down and frowned when she saw that she was in a pair of pink flannel, cloud-covered pajamas. The room was like a cartoon-colored adventure world. There were beanbags, toys, mobiles that twirled from the ceilings, whole shelves of lollipops and fruit, and three drinking fountains sticking out from the wall with Raspberry, Lemonade, and Orange Juice written on top of them.

"What is this place?" she whispered to herself. "And where's my backpack?"

Frantically, Max looked around her and saw the pack sitting on a table next to her. She picked it up, and after going through it, was relieved to see that everything was still there, including her notebook.

Then she remembered.

She'd been kidnapped!

Not only that, there was someone asleep in a bed across the room! She put her backpack on, stood up, took a super-large, round, rainbow-colored lollipop from a shelf nearby, and tiptoed over to the other bed. She wasn't going to be kidnapped without letting them know how much trouble she could be.

She stood by the bed and held the lollipop up high.

"Okay, you kidnapper, take this!" she cried.

Max brought the lollipop down just as the person in the bed rolled over and only narrowly avoided being hit.

"Hey, what are you doing? Can't a person get a little sleep?" someone said from under the blankets.

Max knew that voice.

"Linden? Is that you?" she asked.

"Who else do you think it is?" he mumbled.

"I thought you were a kidnapper." Max shrugged, holding the lollipop against her chest and feeling a little guilty.

Linden threw the covers off his face.

"A little relaxed for a kidnapper, don't you think?"

"Sorry," Max apologized.

Linden sat up.

"I could have been killed by a giant lollipop. I was hoping for a more glamorous ending to my life," he said.

Max put the lollipop down and rubbed her forehead as she sat down on the bed next to him.

"I feel like someone's been using my head for a football."

"Yeah, me too," said Linden. "Whoever grabbed us must have given us something to knock us out."

Max suddenly looked worried.

"Who do you think they are? What do you think they want with us?"

"I'm not sure," said Linden. "But from what Francis and Valerie said about Mr. Blue, I'm sure that he's involved somehow and that it's no accident that it happened just as we found the Time and Space Retractor Meter."

Max took out her notebook and tried to think calmly.

"Okay, here's how things stand. We're trapped in a house, location unknown. We've been kidnapped by strangers, separated from the only people we know in this country and," Max looked at her watch, "we've got about three hours left before we need to be back home."

"Not only that," said Linden, looking down at his clothes in horror, "I'm wearing bright blue pajamas with toy trains on them."

Max glared at Linden.

"I hardly think what you're wearing is . . ."

Max was interrupted by the door opening. A woman dressed in a smart suit walked in.

"I'm Ms. Peckham," she said gently with a friendly smile.

Max leaped off the bed and threw her hands on her hips. There were so many things that she was angry about, she wasn't sure where to start, but realizing she did feel silly in the pink pajamas, she began there. "Where are my clothes?"

"In the wash. They got a little grubby during your journey here, and I thought you'd feel more comfortable in those."

"I was very comfortable in what I had on before."

"You'll get them back soon, but first Mr. Blue would like to see you."

Suddenly what Max was wearing didn't seem important.

"He would, would he? Well, I'd like to see him too. I've got a few things to tell him."

Linden tried to reach for Max's sleeve to tell her to calm down, but she stepped away from him and stalked out of the room. Seconds later she reappeared, remembering she had no idea where she was, and glowered at Ms. Peckham.

"I guess you'll have to lead the way," she said.

"Certainly, but I suggest you put your slippers on first. It can get cold on the marble floors," said Ms. Peckham as she picked up two pairs of slippers.

One pair were shaped like fluffy yellow ducks, while the other pair were two baby bears.

Linden sighed. "This is going to do nothing for my reputation as a man of fashion."

It was hard to know who Max was more angry at, Mr. Blue or Linden. Unfazed, Linden put on his slippers and backpack and did everything he could not to catch Max's eye.

Outside the room, there was a small humming machine that looked like a mini-hovercraft waiting for them.

Max and Linden stared.

"This is our Mobile People Mover. Or MPM. It's really quite safe," smiled Ms. Peckham. "And it is a bit of a way."

Max and Linden looked at each other. They weren't sure whether to trust her, but knew they had little choice. Max shrugged her shoulders and stepped into the MPM. Linden followed, and they held onto the sides, not knowing what to expect. Ms. Peckham got in after them and, with a gentle whirring sound, the MPM took off and sailed across the floor and up to the high ceilings like a small glider.

"This is awesome!" said Linden.

The MPM sailed through brightly lit corridors filled with sensors that opened and closed doors as they approached. Television screens as flat as paper were hung every few yards along the walls, and robotic arms moved out from the walls to do everything from water plants to open and close curtains. There were also vending machines snugly nestled into walls containing everything from lollipops to hot snacks, drinks, and even games. At the end of one corridor, they glided into a large, glass-roofed area that resembled an overgrown greenhouse with trees, birds, and, amazingly, a waterfall.

"This is Mr. Blue's nature reserve. If you look closely enough, you'll see a giant panda and her baby," said Ms. Peckham proudly. "Mr. Blue is a great lover of animals and is one of the few people to successfully breed pandas in captivity. He is on the verge of completing a series of experiments that will hopefully bring pandas back from the brink of extinction."

Animal conservation! This didn't sound like the evil Mr. Blue that Max and Linden had been told about.

The MPM then turned and headed for the lip of the waterfall.

Linden yelled, "Watch out! We're going to crash!"

Ms. Peckham smiled at them and said, "Hold on."

Max and Linden grabbed onto each other and closed their eyes.

Max shouted, "I know it's a bad time, Linden, but there's something I want to tell you."

"What did you say?" Linden yelled back.

"There's something I want to tell you," Max shouted again, as the thundering wash of the water came closer and closer.

"I can't hear you," Linden cried.

But it was too late. Just then Max and Linden screamed as the MPM headed straight into the waterfall.

MR. BLUE

CHAPTER 16

Vats of Green Jelly
and a Zillion Trillion
Million Dollars

When they came to a standstill, Max and Linden opened their eyes and saw Ms. Peckham standing on a shiny metal platform next to their hovering MPM.

"I told you it was perfectly safe, and here we are," she beamed.

Max and Linden realized they hadn't died in the waterfall, and tried to take in their new surroundings. They were high above the ground in a giant metallic room that looked like a darkened aircraft hangar. Behind Ms. Peckham was a large, silver door that seemed to be vibrating with a pulsing light. There were no walls, just the door with a camera fixed above it, a platform, and a seemingly endless abyss on either side. Nothing else could be seen except a window of light above them, which they assumed was the back of the waterfall they had just navigated.

"But how . . ." began Linden.

"With this," said Ms. Peckham, holding out a small electronic device. "Just before we passed through the waterfall, I activated the hydrogen atoms in the water so that they stood aside. That's why we aren't wet, to answer your question."

Linden's mouth fell open. "Come in," said Ms. Peckham, gesturing toward the door.

As Max and Linden stepped out of the MPM onto the platform, the camera followed their every move. Ms. Peckham put her palm against the door. The light coming from it pulsated strongly before it opened, as if it had read her palmprint as some kind of identity pass.

Max was impressed, but tried as hard as she could not to show it.

"This Mr. Blue has got a lot of explaining to do," said Max, as she waited for Ms. Peckham to lead the way.

Linden moved close behind her.

"Max, can you do me a favor?" he asked. "We are talking about an evil mastermind here. Can you avoid saying anything that's going to upset him?"

Max kept walking.

"As if I'd do that," she said, raising her eyebrows.

"Follow me," said Ms. Peckham, still beaming.

Max wondered how anyone could smile so much.

As they followed Ms. Peckham through the door and down a dimly lit, metal passageway, Max leaned next to Linden.

"Do you still have that recording device that Ella gave you?" she whispered.

"It's a CTR."

"Whatever. Have you got it?"

"Yeah. It's in my pack," Linden replied.

"Switch it on," said Max. "We might need it later."

Linden felt around in his pack and turned on the CTR.

They reached another door that again opened when Ms. Peckham placed her hand on it. Inside was what looked like a brightly colored amusement park. There were TV monitors and video screens everywhere, and all the latest consoles and games, including some that neither Max nor Linden had seen before. Lining the walls were shelves containing the largest selection of DVDs that they'd ever seen, including all of Linden's favorites.

"There's *Batman*, *Indiana Jones*, *Mission Impossible*, old and new versions." Linden walked over to them. "I could stay here forever."

"Well, we don't have forever," said Max, grabbing his wrist.

A bright red chair swung around and a smiling man sat behind a large wooden desk, staring at them. Two familiar-looking men stood at his side.

"Sorry about the unusual invitation to my home," the seated man said in a smooth TV advertisement voice. "It may have seemed a little abrupt, but it was necessary for everyone's safety."

He picked up a plate from the table beside him and held it out to them.

"Raspberry doughnut," he offered.

Linden's stomach rumbled at the sight of the doughnut, and Max put her hands on her hips.

"What I'd like is an explanation," she said. "Starting with who you are."

"Of course, first things first. Please, have a seat," he said.

169

Linden's face fell as the man put the plate back on the table.

Before Max could protest, he pressed the button of a remote control device on the arm of his seat and two very comfortable chairs rolled across the room from behind them, gently forcing them to sit down.

Max and Linden looked at each other, puzzled.

"Did those chairs just move across the room?" asked Linden.

"I think we have enough to think about without asking that," said Max.

The man took a chocolate bar from his pocket and unwrapped it.

"I am Mr. Blue," he announced, taking a bite of the bar.

Max's and Linden's eyes widened. He was much younger than they expected and looked like a regular guy, not someone who broke up families and wanted to control the world.

Linden looked longingly at the raspberry doughnuts and the chocolate bar.

Mr. Blue smiled.

"Sorry for my rudeness. Maybe you'd like something a little more substantial?"

Mr. Blue clapped his hands. Two chefs in tall white hats walked through the door carrying steaming plates of food, which they placed on the desk between Max, Linden, and Mr. Blue.

Linden nearly fainted from the smell of it.

"Roast lamb and vegetables," he whispered. "My favorite."

Max looked down at her plate and saw her favorite dish, Thai vegetable curry.

How did he know what they liked?

Linden tried to resist, but he hadn't eaten properly in ages. He grabbed his fork and was about to swallow his first mouthful when Max stopped him.

"It might be poisoned!" she warned.

Mr. Blue laughed softly.

"I see you need a little convincing. Let me reassure you."

Mr. Blue took a gold fork from his pocket and tasted both dishes.

"A little too much salt on the lamb, but otherwise they are both perfect."

Linden and Max couldn't wait any longer. They dug in.

Max pointed her fork at Mr. Blue.

"So are you going to tell us why you kidnapped us?" she demanded.

Mr. Blue smiled.

"I think the word *kidnap* is a little harsh. I just wanted to show you my wonderful home." He paused. "And ask you a few questions."

Max put down her fork while Linden kept eating.

"Well, I have a few questions of my own, like what

were your plans for Francis, Ben, and the Time and Space Machine?"

"My plans were very honorable, I assure you. With the Time and Space Machine, we'd be famous all over the world as saviors of humankind. We'd be able to go back in history and stop wars before they happened, go into the future and find cures for diseases, and make the world a better place."

Mr. Blue paused and smiled at Ms. Peckham and his bodyguards.

"Or at least that's what I told Francis and Ben," he laughed.

Max disliked Mr. Blue more and more with each word he said.

"What are your real plans?" she asked.

"To become the richest man in the world by selling the machine to whoever wants to use it."

"Even if they buy it for bad reasons?" asked Max.

"What they do with it after it is theirs is none of my business, my dear," said Mr. Blue with another smile.

"And what do you want with us?" asked Max.

"Oh, Max, I think you're clever enough to know that."

Max froze.

"How did you know my name?" she asked, her brave front slipping a little.

"There are a lot of things I know about you, Maxine Anne Remy. I know your dad lives in L.A. and couldn't be with you over this vacation and that your mom works long hours fussing over famous TV personalities all day instead of you."

Max and Linden looked at each other.

"And Linden, you live in Mindawarra on a farm with your dad, you love Ben and Eleanor like your second parents, and you lost your mother two years ago."

Suddenly Max and Linden lost their appetites.

Mr. Blue examined a fingernail on his right hand as he continued.

"And do you want to know the best part? I know you're going to help me find the Time and Space Retractor Meter because you don't want anything to happen to the families you love so much, do you?"

He looked up sharply at Max.

She was shaken but didn't want to let Mr. Blue know it.

"So you really are the slime bag we were told you were," she snarled.

Mr. Blue looked offended.

"Now that's not very nice. It's just business, Maxine."

"It's Max and I'm not doing business with you!" she shouted.

Linden looked worried.

"Max, be careful," he whispered.

Mr. Blue's smile dropped. He looked carefully at Max so that she felt uneasy and shifted in her seat.

"You and I have a lot in common, Max. We're not the kind of people who give up easily," he said in a quiet voice that had a scary edge to it.

173

"For years I have been trailing Francis to get the Time and Space Retractor Meter, but it seemed nothing I had would tempt him to help me. Until now."

Mr. Blue stared at Max and Linden like they were two freshly cooked chickens and he was savoring the moment when he would devour them. He clicked his fingers and the men in suits moved closer.

"Take them to the Jelly Room and see if that won't convince them to cooperate. And make sure Francis Williams knows where they are."

Max was furious. She hated being pushed around by anyone, and even though she was facing one of the meanest, most powerful men in the world, she wasn't about to let him have it all his way.

"I'm not going anywhere until I've changed," she declared, crossing her arms against her chest.

"Max, be careful," Linden cautioned out of the corner of his mouth.

"I'm sorry?" Mr. Blue asked quizzically.

"I'm not going anywhere until I've changed back into my own clothes. You can do the tough-guy act all you like, but your brain's completely turned to mush if you think I'm going anywhere dressed like this."

Linden saw Mr. Blue's eyes light up with anger, as if someone had lit two little warning flares in them.

"Maybe we could just go as we are," suggested Linden, thinking that if Max didn't stop, they were going to end up somewhere a lot worse than the Jelly Room.

Max stared at Mr. Blue as he stood before her with his eyebrows raised. No one had ever spoken to him like this, and here was an eleven-year-old girl doing just that. As much as she annoyed him, there was something about Max that Mr. Blue had to admire.

"Fine, Maxine. You may change, but it won't make a scrap of difference to where you're going. Take them away."

Max and Linden struggled as they were carried outside and back to their rooms to change clothes. Then they were led down a long corridor and into an elevator that seemed to take forever to stop. When the doors opened, they were herded into a round room with a huge vat of green jelly in the center.

"The MPM was a much smoother way to travel," said Linden, as he was jostled forward by the guard.

In the Jelly Room, the guards made them sit on a small metal plank so that their backpacks leaned against each other. They tied their hands behind them with thick rope that they then circled around both their waists. The plank was hoisted up so that they were suspended high above the vat of jelly.

Mr. Blue walked in, his hands clasped behind his back. "Have you ever eaten green jelly?" he asked calmly.

"I never was a big fan," said Linden.

"This jelly has been found to absorb a formula of ours

more readily than other foodstuffs, which enables us to control the thoughts of the young children who eat it," explained Mr. Blue. "Could have lots of advantages in the future. Children are such unpredictable creatures. But back to the jelly. It has a soothing feel at first, but after a while it's like you're being eaten by the blob and you just sink."

Max stared Mr. Blue in the eye.

"Let me tell you what is going to happen," he continued.

"Do you have to?" said Linden, not sure he wanted to hear the gory details of his imminent demise.

Mr. Blue smiled.

"Oh, but it's my favorite part. In ten minutes, you will be lowered slowly toward the jelly. In half an hour the jelly will begin to sink into your shoes, then rise to your trousers, then up to your necks, soaking into your clothes and leaving a pleasant yet strangely sticky feeling all over you. Then, a short while after that, you will be swimming. And if Francis doesn't respond to my call, a short while after that, you will be a permanent fixture of green."

Mr. Blue and his guards laughed and turned to leave.

"I'll let you think about that," Mr. Blue called over his shoulder as the door closed behind him.

Max looked down at the jelly and started to breathe quickly.

"Linden," she gasped.

"What?" he asked.

"I'm afraid of heights," she whispered.

"The best way to stay calm is to not look down. And to think about something else," said Linden. "Like whether the recording device worked. If we got all that Mr. Blue said to us, we can use it to finally convince the government that he is evil. You just have to try and get it out of my bag. It's in the side pocket."

He wriggled around so that Max could get a better angle to reach for it. She twisted her hands in the rope, moving closer and closer to the side pocket. After a bit more maneuvering, she had it. She held it carefully so as not to drop it into the jelly.

"Is it working?" she asked, holding it out so Linden could get to it.

Linden strained his neck hard so that he could see the CTR in Max's hands. He wriggled his fingers to the buttons and after rewinding the tape, pressed play.

"My plans were very honorable, I assure you. With the Time and Space Machine, we'd be famous all over the world as saviors of humankind. We'd be able to go back in history and stop wars before they happened, go into the future and find cures for diseases and make the world a better place. Or at least that's what I told Francis and Ben."

"It worked!" Linden said excitedly.

"That's great," said Max, who accidentally glanced at the jelly again.

"Max, are you okay?" Linden asked.

"Yeah," she said. "Except we're going to die!"

"Will you stop looking down!" Linden cried.

Max looked up, but she was still breathing fast.

Linden thought hard about how he could make her calm.

"If you could get rid of any vegetable in the world, what would it be?" he asked.

Max scowled.

"What?"

"If you could get rid of any vegetable in the world, what would it be?" Linden repeated.

"I don't know," she said, thinking Linden had lost it.

"Nobody likes every vegetable. Even you. Now, what would it be?"

Max thought about it.

"Cabbage," she said, breathing a little slower.

"I'd get rid of brussel sprouts," said Linden. "I've never seen the point of those, and I have to have a dad who grows them."

Linden went on.

"If you won a zillion trillion million dollars, what would you do with it?"

"Buy the biggest bar of chocolate I could," said Max quickly.

"Chocolate? But you're a health freak," said Linden.

"I know, but when I'm worried I like to eat chocolate," explained Max.

Linden tried to think of another question.

"If you could change one thing about yourself, what would it be?" he asked.

Max thought about this one.

"Anything?" she asked.

"Anything," said Linden.

Max thought some more.

"I'd have a mother and father who both lived with me," she said in a much calmer voice.

"Yeah, me too," he said quietly.

"Max, what was it you wanted to say to me before we went through the waterfall?"

"Oh, I just wanted to say . . ." Max began, but she was interrupted as the suspension bridge suddenly jerked downwards.

"What's happening?" she shouted, panicking again.

"We're being lowered toward the jelly," cried Linden.

Max screamed.

"This is the end, Max!"

CHAPTER 17

A Deal with the Devil

In his office, Mr. Blue sat with Ms. Peckham and his body-guards over cups of tea.

"Not long now and I'll have the vital component I need to create history," smirked Mr. Blue. "Once the Time and Space Machine is finished, everyone will want it and we'll become the richest people in the world. Governments will want it to build economies and win elections, prisoners will want it to escape to safety in another era, rich people will want to take exotic vacations. I don't care what they use it for, as long as I make lots of money."

Mr. Blue, Ms. Peckham, and the bodyguards laughed, while on the wall behind them, a monitor displayed the scared faces of Linden and Max being lowered toward the vat of green jelly.

Ms. Peckham's mobile phone rang.

"Hello?"

There was a pause while Ms. Peckham listened.

"Send him up," she said and turned to Mr. Blue. "Not long now until the past, present, and future of the world is ours."

The door opened and Francis entered the room.

"How wonderful to see you again, Francis."

Mr. Blue stood up and held out his hand.

Francis didn't move.

"Where are Max and Linden?" he said, his face looking stern.

"They're busy for the moment, which gives us a chance

to catch up and talk about old times," said Mr. Blue.

"I didn't come here to talk. I came to get Max and Linden," said Francis. "They have no business with you!"

"Oh, but they do." Mr. Blue added with a smarmy grin, "Let me show you."

Mr. Blue pointed to the monitor where Francis saw Linden and Max dangling less than three feet above the jelly and getting lower each minute.

Francis lunged at Mr. Blue but the bodyguards stepped in front and held him back.

"They haven't done anything! What do you want with them?" yelled Francis.

Mr. Blue sat down in his chair and took a sip of his tea.

"Oh, I think you know that, Francis," he said. "You're going to hand over the Time and Space Retractor Meter or Max and Linden will be on tonight's menu as dessert."

Francis tried to wrestle free from the guards but they were too strong for him.

"You only want the machine so you can use it for your evil, scheming purposes," he shouted.

"Evil is in the eye of the beholder," said Mr. Blue with a sickly sweet smile.

Francis stared at the monitor, not knowing what to do. He had to save Linden and Max before they drowned in the vat of jelly, but he also knew that if Mr. Blue got his hands on the Time and Space Retractor Meter, the world would never be the same again.

Mr. Blue turned to the bodyguards.

"Take him down to the Jelly Room where he can enjoy the show up close. Maybe that will convince him to help me."

The guards dragged Francis away.

"You'll never get away with this, Blue!" Francis shouted.

CHAPTER 18

A Very Slimy End

"We're going to die!" screamed Max for what seemed like the hundreth time.

"Don't you have anything more useful to say?" asked Linden, sick of hearing her predict their end.

"Not when we're going to die!" Max yelled.

She'd really lost it this time, Linden realized, as their shoes reached the top of the green jelly. It couldn't end like this. Not after they'd come so far and gotten so close to completing Mission Matter Transporter.

Again, he struggled to think of what they could do.

Why not use the CTR to call the top security forces in England so they could rescue them! But he didn't know the number or how they would find Mr. Blue's hideout.

He did know Ella's number though!

"Max?" asked Linden.

"We're going to die," sighed Max, watching the jelly seep into her favorite pair of blue running shoes.

"No we won't, I've got an idea," said Linden. "We can get Ella to rescue us."

Max stopped panicking and turned her head toward Linden.

"Well isn't she just great?" said Max sarcastically.

"What is your problem with Ella?" demanded Linden.

Max thought hard.

"She . . . she . . ." Max floundered.

"Well?" asked Linden.

"She flirted with you and wasted our time when we had important work to do."

"You're jealous!" Linden said.

"Me?" Max laughed. "Jealous?"

"Yeah, and the sooner you get over it the better because the jelly has reached almost up to our shins."

Max looked down, saw the jelly soaking into her jeans, and forgot all about Ella.

"We're going to die!" she called out.

Linden pressed the button on the CTR that sent a signal to Ella.

He waited a few seconds before a signal came back and he heard Ella's voice.

"Linden, where are you?" she asked frantically.

"We're at Mr. Blue's hideout," said Linden.

"It works!" shouted Max. "That's great!"

"Are you okay?" asked Ella, sounding worried.

"I've been in more friendly places," said Linden, trying not to let on that they were about to become giant jelly babies.

"We just need to talk for a few minutes to give the CTR a chance to get a reading of where you are," said Ella.

"We want you to do something first," said Linden. "We've got a recording of Mr. Blue that will prove to the world he is a fake. Is there any way we can get it to you?"

The jelly soaked up to Max's and Linden's knees as they listened to Ella's instructions.

"Each recording is saved as a document," explained Ella. "Enter the number of the document and using the main menu press *transfer*."

Linden did what Ella said and the communication device hummed as it transferred the recording.

"Got it!" Ella cried.

"Take it to the top security forces as soon as you can, and we'll finally stop Mr. Bluc in his tracks," said Linden. "Has the reading of our location come through yet?"

"Nothing. Mr. Blue may have put some kind of magnetic force around his hideout to stop detection by devices such as radars and the CTR," said Ella.

"At least we've got him on tape," said Linden.

"Yeah. Mom and I will get it to the right people as soon as we can. Then we'll see you soon," she said hopefully.

"We'll be gone," said Linden sadly.

"Oh," said Ella, unable to hide her disappointment.

"We've got to get back to America. But I'll talk to you when we get there," Linden added.

"I'll miss you," said Ella.

"Me too," Linden replied quietly. "Bye."

Just then the door opened and Francis, with his arms held behind his back, was hustled into the room by the two bodyguards. Linden quickly turned off the CTR and tucked it into his pocket.

"Francis! You came!" shouted Max.

The bodyguards stood over Francis.

"When you're ready to help, just press this button here and the kids will be saved," said one of the guards, pointing to a large red button on the wall.

"It's all up to you, Mr. Professor," they sneered as they left the room.

Francis was shocked to see how deep in the jelly Max and Linden were.

"I'm sorry I got you kids mixed up in this," he said. "We have to find a way of getting you out of here."

Max's face brightened, knowing exactly what Alex Crane would do in a situation like this.

"That depends," she said as the jelly squelched up to her waist. "Are you ready for a big trip?"

Linden smiled excitedly, knowing what Max was thinking.

"We could use the Matter Transporter to take us home."

Max looked at Francis.

"That's if you want to," she said quietly.

"That way we escape from here, keep the Time and Space Machine from Mr. Blue and get back to the farm before Ben and Eleanor miss us," cried Linden.

They sank deeper into the jelly as Francis's face grimaced in trying to decide what to do.

"Only we have to go now," said Max.

Francis saw the jelly rise still higher.

"Let's do it!" he said.

"Do you have the Retractor Meter with you?" asked Max.

"It's somewhere safe," Francis replied, pointing to the sole of his left shoe.

Linden and Max beamed.

"Now for the control panel," Linden said.

Max whispered instructions to Linden over her shoulder. "See if you can reach into my bag and get it."

Linden managed to do as she said and maneuvered the panel out, holding it so Max could see it.

"How does it look?" he asked nervously.

The red light beeped faintly.

"The signal's really weak," said Max.

She looked at Francis. "Do you think it will work?"

"If Ben has made it following our plans, it will be fine as long as the jelly hasn't short-circuited the initialization panel," said Francis.

Max, Linden, and Francis looked worried.

"We have to try," said Linden.

Max's fingers wriggled toward the rod at the side of the control panel.

"Can you hold it out a little more?" she asked Linden. "I can't quite see the screen."

Linden forced his hands to stretch as far as the rope would let him toward Max. An image of the room appeared before her on the LED screen and she did her best to draw an outline with the plastic rod around her, Linden, and Francis.

"Done," she said breathlessly. "You might feel a bit of tingling when you make contact with the transporter capsule, but you'll be fine," Max explained to Francis.

She moved the rod onto the *activate* key. There was a small *zap* sound and a quick flash of light. Francis held his arm out in front of him as sparks ricocheted around him. His eyes brightened.

"Ben, you did it," he said quietly.

Linden held the control panel above the rising jelly. Max tried not to panic as she used the rod to type Ben and Eleanor's address in Pennsylvania.

"See you all when we get there," she said.

"Happy flying," said Linden, trying to smile, but worrying that transporting all three of them with a weak power signal was probably very risky.

"Ready? Three, two, one."

Max took a deep breath and brought the rod down onto the *transport* key.

The room shook and filled with noise. There was the whirring sound that got louder and louder, echoing off the walls of the Jelly Room. Max and Linden closed their eyes as the jelly wobbled around them and swirled across the room in a cyclone of green flying particles.

There was an explosion of sound and light.

And then they were gone.

⊕

Ms. Peckham's eyes widened as she stared at the monitor.

"Mr. Blue, I think you should see this," she said.

Mr. Blue walked over to the monitor. He was smiling.

"Have they finally decided to give themselves up?" he beamed.

"Not quite," said Ms. Peckham shakily.

Mr. Blue looked at the monitor and the smile fell from his face like a brick.

"Where are they?" he asked, his voice shaking with anger.

"They just," Ms. Peckham struggled to find the right word, "disappeared."

"Disappeared!" shouted Mr. Blue. "They can't just have disappeared!"

He turned to the two bodyguards, who shrugged their shoulders.

"Find them!" he barked. "Or you'll end up in something far worse than a vat of jelly!"

Mr. Blue's face went beet red as the guards backed out of the room.

"If Francis and those kids have escaped, this will not be the last they hear of me," he said to Ms. Peckham. "The day they met me will haunt them forever!"

CHAPTER 19

Home Sweet Home

"Boy, you really panicked back there."

Max opened her eyes and saw Linden and Ralph standing over her.

"Where am I?" asked Max, frowning and trying to remember what had happened.

"Same place as me," said Linden. "On Ben and Eleanor's farm. Only I landed on a few bales of hay and you landed in Larry's feed trough."

Max looked around her.

"Urghh! Why is it me who always has the smelly landings?"

Linden smiled. "Ben really needs to iron out those hiccups before you land in too many more stinky situations."

Max wasn't impressed.

"Just help me out," she said.

Ralph barked and licked Max on the nose.

"Not you. I said Linden."

Ralph whined.

"Max is excited to see you, Ralph," said Linden sarcastically. "She just has a funny way of showing it."

Linden helped Max out of the trough.

"Do you still think we're going to die?" Linden asked.

Then Max remembered where they'd escaped from.

"I know I seemed a little worried back there," she stammered, "but I always thought we'd get back safely."

Linden frowned at Max as she tried to pick bits of Larry's food and green jelly from her hair and clothes.

After all they'd been through, he still didn't understand girls.

Or at least this girl.

Then Max remembered something else.

"Where's Francis?" she asked.

Linden turned around.

"Somewhere very cosy if you ask me."

Max followed Linden's eyes and saw Francis asleep in a rocking chair on the verandah.

"Should we wake him up?" asked Linden.

"No. I've got a better idea," said Max with a smile and she walked towards the house.

"I hope it involves breakfast," said Linden to himself.

Later, after they'd washed away the green jelly and changed their clothes, Max and Linden stood in the kitchen and heard Ben and Eleanor's bedroom door open.

"Here they come!" whispered Max excitedly.

They could barely stop shaking with excitement as Ben and Eleanor walked into the kitchen.

Linden flung the screen door open and invited everyone outside.

"Linden and I have someone we want you to meet," Max said.

Francis stepped forward and Ben's smile melted away as if he'd seen a ghost.

"Francis? Is that you?" Ben asked quietly, thinking his eyes and the sun were playing tricks on him.

"It was the last time I looked in the mirror," Francis answered. "But a lot has happened over the past few hours."

Ben looked at his brother and a smile spread across his face like jam across toast.

"It's good to see you, Francis. Now come here."

Ben gave him a big hug. Then Eleanor hugged Francis, and Ben hugged Eleanor, and everyone got pretty teary.

Including Max.

Linden looked at her.

"You're not crying, are you?" he asked.

Max wiped her eyes.

"No. The sun's making my eyes water."

Linden smiled at her.

"You're really something, Max Remy. And you know what? I think we make a good team. Next time you have a spy mission, I'm your man."

Max felt like she wanted to cry even more.

"It's great to see you, but how did you get here?" said Ben to Francis.

Francis looked at Max and Linden.

"Why don't we talk about it over breakfast," he said. "It's a long story."

After they piled back into the kitchen, Eleanor filled the table with food and drink. Francis, Max, and Linden explained everything that had happened. Landing in London, finding Valerie and Ella, riding on the Mobile

People Mover, sinking in the vat of jelly, and meeting Ms. Peckham and Mr. Blue.

Ben wasn't happy about Linden and Max using the Matter Transporter, especially after he'd told Max it wasn't ready to transport people. He also told them that what they did was dangerous and they could have been hurt, but he couldn't stay angry at them. The transporter had worked and, for the first time in years, Francis was back with them.

"Let's make a toast," said Ben, raising his orange juice. "To Francis, who I waited too long to see again."

"To Francis," they all said as they clinked their glasses.

"And to Linden and Max, two of the bravest kids I know," said Ben proudly.

The glasses were clinked again as Max and Linden looked at each other and smiled.

There was a lot to catch up on, and as everyone talked and laughed and listened to each other's stories, Eleanor put her arm around Max.

"You're a very special person Max Remy, you know that?" she whispered. "Life around here will never be the same again because of you."

Max blushed and thought about what had happened since she had come to the farm. She looked around the kitchen with everyone talking and laughing and eating, and realized that she felt more at home here than she had anywhere else in her life.

When they had finished, Max and Linden suddenly

felt exhausted and almost fell asleep at the table.

"I think it's time for our two top spies to get to bed," said Ben.

Max and Linden dragged themselves up from the table.

"Do you think that you and Francis will finish the Time and Space Machine now?" asked Max.

Ben and Francis looked at each other.

"We'll have to talk about that. For now you two get some rest," said Ben. He gave her a big hug and said good night.

When they were in their beds, Max turned to Linden.

"Linden, you're right. We are a good team, and I wouldn't want to work with anyone else. I also want to tell you what I was going to say before we went through the waterfall."

Max took a deep breath.

"I've never had a best friend before, but now that I've met you I know what it's like. The pact we made before we used the Matter Transporter was one of the nicest things anyone's ever said to me. And even though I don't say it very often, you're really okay, you know, for a boy and everything, and I hope we stay friends for a really long time."

There was a pause.

"Linden? Did you hear me?"

Max stepped over to Linden's bed and lifted the blankets off his face.

He was sound asleep.

Max smiled.

"Maybe I'll tell you another time," she said.

Max yawned and climbed back into bed.

She dreamed of spies and missions and Alex Crane, Superspy from Spy Force.

CHAPTER 20

A Message from **SPY FORCE**

Eleanor stepped onto the back verandah and called out, "Max, Linden? Where are you?"

"Why am I even asking?" she mumbled. "Like I don't know the answer to that myself."

Eleanor walked down to the shed and knocked on the door.

Nothing.

She knocked again.

Still nothing.

"Sometimes I wonder if they even remember I'm here," she said. Ever since Francis had arrived some weeks before, the four of them had spent most of their days in Ben's shed.

She turned the handle and slowly pushed the door open to see Ben, Francis, Linden, and Max leaning over a small contraption with buttons, dials, knobs, and flashing lights.

"Max and Linden, there's a letter for you," said Eleanor, handing it over. "And it looks important."

Max took the letter and opened it.

Her eyes widened.

"It's from Spy Force!"

"What?" Linden asked. "I thought you made that up?"

"So did I," Max exclaimed.

"What does it say?" asked Ben.

Max read it out loud.

Dear Max and Linden,
On behalf of **SPY FORCE**, the Secret

Government Security Agency, we would like to extend to you our gratitude for helping to uncover the illicit activities within the Department of Science and New Technologies. Your service to this country and the world has been invaluable.

Yours truly,
R. R. Steinberger
Administrative Manager
SPY FORCE

"Wow!" said Linden. "There really is a Spy Force!"

"And they seem to think you've done a pretty good thing," said Francis. "My guess is that Mr. Blue is no longer at the department."

"Where do you think he is?" Max asked.

"Somewhere far from us, I hope," said Eleanor.

"The world would be a better place if he just disappeared forever," said Ben.

"I don't think there's much chance of that," said Max. "Mr. Blue doesn't give up easily."

A ringing sound came from Linden's pocket.

"It's the CTR," said Linden, his hands bolting into his pocket like lightning.

Max, suspecting it was Ella, rolled her eyes.

"Really, now how can you tell that?"

Linden missed the sarcasm and excused himself as he walked outside to take the call.

"Ella, hi!" Max heard him say.

Max folded the letter before putting it into her pocket. All the excitement she'd felt before melted away as she listened to Linden's voice, which was a combination of pauses, laughter, and excitement as he talked about the Time and Space Machine and how it was nearly finished, the letter from Spy Force, and other things Max couldn't quite hear because he turned away and lowered his voice.

Eleanor saw Max's face fall and attempted to cheer her up.

"Who would have known we'd have a famous spy in our house?" she asked.

Max tried to smile, but she was too busy listening to what she could hear of the rest of Linden's conversation.

When Linden finished, he came back inside the shed.

"That was Ella," he said excitedly.

"Who?" asked Max, as if she didn't know.

"Ella," Linden replied. "She got a letter too and guess what else? The tape was the vital piece of evidence needed to help Spy Force finally prove that Mr. Blue was evil. He quit his job, saying he wanted to spend more time with his family, but he was really fired, and Valerie reckons the government kept it quiet because if they told the world what he'd been doing, they'd look really stupid."

"Well, you two should be very proud of yourselves," said Ben. "People have been trying to stop Mr. Blue for years."

Linden looked at Max and smiled.

"I guess Mission Matter Transporter was a success?"

"Yeah, I guess it was," said Max.

Eleanor looked at her watch.

"Max, we're going to have to get ready. Your mom will be here soon to pick you up."

Max had forgotten. Today was her last day on the farm.

She looked at the Time and Space Machine and then at Ben and Francis.

"I guess you'll have to finish it without me," she said sadly. They had been working so hard on it over the past few weeks, she forgot that it would have to end.

"You'll be the first to know as soon as we get it working," said Francis.

Max smiled and felt a tear in the corner of her eye.

"I'll help you pack," said Linden.

In the house, Linden sat on Max's bed as she started picking up her stuff.

"Do you think you'll come back and stay sometime?"

"I don't know," said Max. "Would you like me to?"

"Sure," said Linden. "We haven't had a summer this exciting for years."

"Do you think we might get to do another mission together?" asked Max.

"Yep!" said Linden confidently. "Now that Spy Force has our names, we'll be called to help out in other missions for sure."

Max smiled as she folded clothes and squeezed shoes and books into her bag.

There was a pause before Linden said, "And I wouldn't want to work with anyone else."

Max blushed.

"Neither would I," she said.

Linden could feel his face go red too. Then there was another awkward pause as he twisted the tassels on the end of Max's chenille bedspread.

"Max?" he asked. "Can I ask you something?"

"Sure," she said.

"How do you know when you really like someone?"

Max kept packing and avoided looking at him. She tried to remember what she'd heard from her mother, and things she'd read in books and seen in films.

"You feel like you're walking ten feet off the ground all the time. You can't concentrate on anything and you start saying weird kinds of things, like someone else has taken over your brain."

"That's exactly how I feel!" said Linden.

Max blushed again, but this time she was sure she was redder than she'd ever been.

She remembered the first time she'd met Linden and how he had looked like a real wildboy. Who'd have thought that they would be talking about liking each other six weeks later.

"Ella's really cool!" said Linden, smiling and thinking about the last time he saw her.

Max stopped packing.

"Ella?" she frowned.

"Yeah, she's really amazing. She said to say hello to you too."

Max looked away and pushed her pajamas into her bag before zipping it up.

"That's great," she said.

They heard a horn beep and a car drive into the yard.

"That must be Mom," she said quietly.

"I'll miss you," Linden said.

"You'll get over it," said Max, trying to smile.

"Hey," said Linden. "That was a joke."

"Yeah," said Max. "I'm thinking of being a comedienne when I'm not spying."

Linden and Max smiled.

Outside, she heard the slam of a car door and stilted voices buzzing like flies as her mother desperately tried to find something to say to her sister. All the while, Max knew she was itching to leave as soon as possible and was wondering where on earth her daughter could be. Her mom could talk to most people as if she'd swallowed a dictionary.

Words just poured out of her in one giant flood. But when it came to her own family, they dried up like dust in her mouth, making her look really uncomfortable.

"Max, I'm here."

Max thought it would be about three and a half minutes before she ran out of small talk. A bit of a record for her mom under the circumstances.

"Gotta go," said Max as she picked up her bags and her folder of writing.

Outside, her mother was looking at her watch as Max walked down the steps. Something inside Max burned when she saw this.

"Oh, there you are, sweetie," her mother said. "We have to get a move on because I need to be back in the city for an appointment."

Her mother gave her a quick kiss on the cheek and loaded her bags into the car.

Max sighed. Nothing much has changed, she thought.

Ben, Francis, and Eleanor walked toward them and stood nearby.

"Thanks for looking after Max. I hope she wasn't too much trouble," said her mom.

"None at all," said Eleanor. "Would you like to come in for some lunch?"

Max's mother looked at her watch again and seemed as anxious as if someone had dropped a jar of ants down her long, velvet skirt. "I'd love to, but we've got to fly."

Typical, Max thought. *She never has time for anyone except herself and her work.*

She turned to Ben and Eleanor.

"Thanks for the best vacation I've ever had. I'll never forget you," she said.

Ben gave her a hug.

"You have to promise that you'll come back whenever you can," he said.

"And don't wait too long," said Eleanor, brushing Max's hair from her face and giving her a kiss.

"Besides, you'll have to come back to see the machine when it's finished," said Francis.

As they hugged, Francis whispered in her ear, "I was a very unhappy man until I met you and Linden. Thank you."

"Okay, sweetheart. Let's go," said Max's mom, trying to hurry her along.

Max ignored her mother and walked over to Linden and Ralph.

"I've got something for you," said Max.

She opened her folder and handed Linden a small book titled *The Adventures of Alex Crane, Superspy. Chapter One. Mission: The Time and Space Machine.*

Linden smiled.

"It's all about us and the mission," Max explained.

"Thanks." And for once, Linden didn't know what else to say.

"Max?" said her mother with rising impatience in her voice.

"Bye, Ralph," Max said, and patted him on the head. "My master's calling."

"Another joke," said Linden. "You should be careful—this could become a habit."

Max got into the car and watched Ben, Eleanor, Francis, and Linden wave good-bye.

She thought about the summer, the mission, and the people she'd met. Toby Jennings, school, and her home in New York seemed like another galaxy away. She watched the farm getting smaller and smaller as the dust rose up behind her mother's sports car.

I'll be back, she thought.

Linden sat on the verandah and started reading.

⊕

Chronicles of Spy Force:
The Chief of Spy Force congratulated Alex for another mission successfully completed.

"Thanks to you, Mr. Blue is safely behind bars and the world can rest easy that he won't be able to have his evil way anymore."

"I don't think that's the last we'll hear of him," said Alex knowingly. "Mr. Blue's as cunning a criminal as I've ever met."

"For now, you deserve a well-earned break," said the Chief. "And Spy Force is happy to send you anywhere in the world for a two-week rest. Just name the place."

Alex thought hard.

"How about Australia?" she said. "I've never been there: the beaches, the sun, the islands."

"I'll get someone to make the arrangements right away," said the Chief happily.

Just then the Chief's secret phone rang.

"Yeah?" he answered.

There was a pause.

Alex watched as his face became serious.

"Okay, we'll get right on it."

The Chief hung up the phone.

"How about London instead? Mr. Blue has escaped."

Printed in the United States
By Bookmasters